A PRICE
WORTH PAYING?

A PRICE WORTH PAYING?

BY

TRISH MOREY

First published in Great Britain 2013
by Mills & Boon, an imprint of Harlequin (UK) Limited.
Large Print edition 2013
Harlequin (UK) Limited, Eton House,
18-24 Paradise Road, Richmond, Surrey TW9 1SR

© Trish Morey 2013

ISBN: 978 0 263 23216 5

Harlequin (UK) policy is to use papers that are natural,
renewable and recyclable products and made from
wood grown in sustainable forests. The logging and
manufacturing process conform to the legal environmental
regulations of the country of origin.

Printed and bound in Great Britain
by CPI Antony Rowe, Chippenham, Wiltshire

A huge heartfelt thank you to Val, Julio,
Matteo and Leti, Lyn and Phil,
for sharing a wonderful part of the world
with such delight and generosity of spirit.
We had a brilliant time with you all in
Spain, although it was way, way too short.
Clearly we will just have to come back!
I hope I have done justice to your fabulous
part of the world and its people.

Heartfelt thanks must also go to
Marion Lennox and Carol Marinelli
and a wonderful place called Maytone
where dreams happen and very often
do come true. This one did:-)

And last but not least, with thanks to
Joanne Grant. Thank you for your
never-ending patience, guidance and
enthusiasm during a year filled with
all kinds of distractions and excitement
and even the odd swim with dolphins.
It's a privilege to know you.
Working with you is the bonus.

Trish

xxx

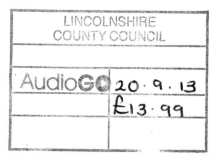

CHAPTER ONE

FELIPE WAS DYING. Six months to live. Maybe twelve at a stretch.

Dying!

Simone swiped away a tear from her cheek, stumbling a little as she ran between the rows of vines clinging to the mountainside. Her grandfather would hate it if he knew she was crying over him. 'I am old,' he'd said, when finally he'd let her learn the truth, 'I've had my time. I have few regrets…' But then his eyes had misted over and she'd seen the enormity of those 'few' regrets swirling in their watery depths.

The sorrow at losing his wife of fifty years to her battle with cancer.

The despair when his recently reconciled daughter and her husband—*Simone's parents*—were lost in a joy flight crash whilst holidaying not three months later.

And the shame of succumbing to drink and then to the cards in the depths of his resultant depression, gambling away three-quarters of the estate before he was discovered and dragged bodily from the table by a friend before he could lose his own home.

It was the regret that was killing him. Oh yes, there was cancer too—that was doing its worst to eat away at his bones and shorten his life—but it was the regret that was sucking away his will to fight his disease and give in to it instead; regret that was telling him that there was no point because he had nothing left to live for.

And nothing anybody could say or do seemed to make a difference. Not when every time he looked out of his window he saw the vines that were no longer his, and he was reminded all over again of all that he had lost.

She stopped at the edge of the estate, where the recently erected fence marked the new border between her grandfather's remaining property and the neighbouring Esquivel estate. Here, where there was a break between the rows of vines staked and trellised high above her head, she could look down over the spectacular coastline of northern Spain. Below her the town of Getaria nestled behind a rocky headland that jutted out into the Bay of Biscay. Beyond that the sea swelled in brilliant shades of blue that changed with the wind and with the sun, a view so unlike what she had at home in Australia that it took her breath away every time she looked at it.

She inhaled deeply of the salt-tinged air, the scene of terraced hills, the tiered vines, the ancient town below all too picture perfect to be real. It wouldn't seem real when she was back home in Melbourne and living again in one of the cheap, outer-city student flats she was used to. But Melbourne and her deferred university studies would have to wait a bit longer. She'd come expecting to stay just a few weeks between semesters. Then Felipe had fallen ill and she'd promised to stay until he was back on his feet. But after this latest news, it was clear she wasn't returning home any time soon. Because there was no way she could leave him now.

Dying.

Hadn't there been enough death lately without losing Felipe too? She was only just getting to know him properly—the long-term rift between him and his daughter keeping the families apart ever since she was a child, Felipe and his wife here in Spain, their wayward daughter, her forbidden lover and their granddaughter living in self-imposed exile in Australia.

All those wasted years, only to be reunited now, when mere months remained.

How could she make those last few months better for Felipe? How to ease the pain of all he had lost? She shook her head, searching for answers as she gazed across the fence at the acres of vines that were once his and that now belonged to others, sensing the enormity of his loss, his guilt, his shame, and wishing there was some way she could make things better.

For there was no way to bring back his wife or his daughter and son-in-law.

There was no money to buy back the acreage he had lost.

And given the long-running rivalry between the two neighbouring families, there was no way the Esquivels were going to hand it back when they had seized such a powerful advantage.

Which left her with only one crazy option.

So crazy there was no way it could ever work.

But was she crazy enough to try?

'You sacked her!' Alesander Manuel Esquivel forgot all about the coffee he was about to pour and glared incredulously at his mother, who stood there with her hands folded meekly in front of her looking as cool and unflurried in the face of his outburst as a quintessential Mother Superior. Her composure only served to feed his outrage. 'What the hell gave you the right to sack Bianca?'

'You were gone the entire month,' Isobel Esquivel countered coolly, 'and you knew what a dreadful housekeeper she was before you left. This apartment was a pigsty. Of course I took the opportunity to sack her and engage a professional cleaner while you were gone. And just look around you,' she said with a flourish of her diamond-encrusted fingers around the now spotless room. 'I don't know how you can possibly be so irritated.'

His mother thought him irritated? Now there was an understatement. After a fifteen-hour flight from California, he'd been looking forward to the simple pleasure of a hot shower before tumbling into bed and tumbling a willing woman beneath him in the process. He suppressed a growl. During her brief tenure, Bianca had proven to be particularly willing.

Finding his mother waiting for him in Bianca's place had not been part of his plans. And so he dredged up a smile to go with the words he knew would irritate his mother right back. 'You know as well as I do, Madre *querida*, that I didn't employ Bianca for her cleaning skills.'

His mother sighed distastefully, turning her face towards the view afforded by the large glass windows that overlooked the Bahia de la Concha, the stunning bay that made San Sebastian famous. 'You don't have to be crude, Alesander,' she said wearily, her back to her son. 'I understand very well why you "*employed*" her. The point is, the longer she was here, the less interested you were in finding a wife.'

'Oh, I assumed finding me a wife was your job.'

Her head snapped back around as the seemingly cool façade cracked. 'This is not a joke, Alesander! You need to face up to your responsibilities. The Esquivel name goes back centuries. Do you intend to let it die out because you are too busy entertaining yourself with the latest *puta-del-dia*?'

'I'm thirty-two years old, Madre. I think my breeding potential might be good for another few years yet.'

'Perhaps, but don't expect Ezmerelda de la Silva to wait for ever.'

'Of course I would expect no such thing. That would be completely unreasonable.'

'It would,' his mother said speculatively, her

eyes narrowing, but nowhere near enough to hide the hopeful sheen that glazed their surface. She took a tentative step closer to her son. 'Do you mean to say you've come to your senses while you've been away and decided to settle down at last?' She gave a tinkling little laugh, the sound so false it all but rattled against the windows. 'Oh, Alesander, you might have said.'

'I mean,' he said, his lips curling at his mother's pointless hopes, 'there is no *point* in Ezmerelda waiting a moment longer when there is no way on this earth that I'm marrying her.'

His mother's expression grew tight and hard as she crossed her arms and turned pointedly back towards the window. 'You know our families have had an understanding ever since you were both children. Ezmerelda is the obvious choice for you.'

'Your choice, not mine!' He would sooner choose a shark for a wife than the likes of Ezmerelda de la Silva. She was a beauty, it was true, and once in his distant past he had been tempted, but he had soon learned there was no warmth to her, no fire, indeed nothing behind the polished façade, nothing but a cold fish who had been raised with the sole imperative to marry well.

Whether married or not, he would settle for nothing less than a hot-blooded woman to share his bed. Was it any wonder he had populated his bed with nothing less?

'So what about grandchildren then?' Isobel pleaded, changing tack, her hand flat over her heart. 'If you won't consider marrying for the sake of the family name, what about for my sake? When will you give me grandchildren of my own?'

It was Alesander's turn to laugh. 'You overplay your hand, Madre. I seem to recall you don't like children all that much. At least, that's how I remember it.'

The older woman sniffed. 'You were raised to be the best,' she said without a hint of remorse. 'You were raised to be strong.'

'Then is it any wonder I wish to make my own decisions?'

His mother suddenly looked so tightly wound he thought she might snap. 'You cannot play this game forever, Alesander, no matter how much you seem to enjoy it. Next week it is Markel de la Silva's sixtieth birthday celebration. Ezmerelda's mother and I were hoping that you might accompany Ezmerelda to the party. Couldn't you at least honour the friendship between our families by doing that much?'

To what end? To have the news of their 'surprise' betrothal announced the same night as some bizarre kind of birthday treat? He wouldn't be surprised. His mother was particularly fond of concocting such treats. She would love to put him on the spot and force the issue.

'How unfortunate. I do believe I'm busy that night.'

'You have to be there! It would be a deliberate snub to the family not to appear.'

He sighed, suddenly tired of the sport of baiting his mother. Because of course he would be there. Markel de la Silva was a good man; a man he respected greatly. It wasn't his fault his daughter took after her grasping mother.

'Of course I will be there. But what part of "there is no way I'm marrying Ezmerelda", did you not understand?'

'Yes, you say that now, but you know there is no one else suitable and sooner or later you will have to fulfil your destiny as sole heir to the Esquivel estate,' his mother said, giving up any pretence that securing a marriage between their two families wasn't her ultimate goal. 'When are you going to realise that?'

'I can't give you the answer you want but, rest assured, Madre, when I do decide to marry, you'll be the first to know.'

His mother left then, all bristling indignation and pursed lips in a perfumed, perfectly coiffed package, her perfume lingering on the air along with his irritation long after she'd gone. He stared out of the same window Isobel had blindly stared out of a short time ago, but the view didn't escape him. Between the mountains Igueldo and Urgull, with its huge statue of Christ looking down and blessing the city, sprouted the wooded Isla de Santa Clara, forming a magnificent backdrop to the finest city beach in Europe.

He'd bought this apartment some years ago sight unseen after yet another argument with his mother. At the time he'd simply wanted a bolt-hole away from the family estate in Getaria, a twenty-minute drive away.

He'd got more than a bolt-hole as it turned out. He'd got the best view in the city. Today the white sandy curve of the bay was less crowded than it had been when he had left a month ago at the height of summer, most tourists content in September's milder weather to promenade around the Concha rather than swim in its protected waters.

His gaze focused in on the beach, the insistent ache in his groin returning. Bianca used to spend her days on the sand, working on her tan. To good effect, if he remembered correctly, even if his mother couldn't see the advantages of long tanned limbs over a spotless floor.

He scanned the beach. Maybe Bianca was

down there right now. He pulled his phone from his pocket and searched for her number. Isobel must have paid her extremely well for her to keep the news of her sudden eviction from him. But if she was still in the area…

Halfway to calling he paused, before repocketing the phone. What was he doing? It was one thing to have her waiting here for him. It was another entirely to go searching for her. Did he really want to give her the wrong idea? After all, she'd been almost at her use-by date as it was.

Bianca had known that. He'd made it plain when she'd started that she'd be looking for another position inside three months. Which probably explained why she'd gone so quietly. Because she'd always known the position was temporary.

Still he growled his displeasure as he tugged at his tie and pushed himself away from the windows. Because on top of having to find himself a new live-in cleaner, it meant that tonight he'd just have to settle for a cold shower.

CHAPTER TWO

IT WASN'T JUST crazy. It was insane.

Simone stood with her back to the bay and looked up at the building where Alesander Esquivel lived and felt cold chills up her spine despite the warm autumn sun. His apartment would have to be on the top floor, of course, and so far above her she wondered that she dared to think he would lower himself long enough to even let her in, let alone seriously consider her proposal.

And why should he, when it was the maddest idea she'd ever had? She'd get laughed out of San Sebastian, probably laughed out of Spain.

She almost turned and fled back along the Playa de la Concha to the bus station and her grandfather's house in Getaria and certain refuge.

Almost.

Except what other choice did she have? Getting laughed out of the city, the country, was better than doing nothing. Doing nothing would mean sitting back and watching her grandfather's life slide inexorably towards death, day by day.

Doing nothing was no choice at all. Not any longer.

How could she not even try?

She swallowed down air, the sea breeze that toyed with the layers of her favourite skirt flavoured with garlic and tomatoes and frying fish from a bayside restaurant. Her stomach rumbled a protest. She could not stand here simply waiting to cross this busy road for ever. Soon she must return to her grandfather's simple house and prepare their evening meal. She had told him she needed to shop for the paella she had planned. He would be wondering why she was taking so long.

And suddenly the busy traffic parted and her legs were carrying her across the road, and the closer she got to the building, the larger and more imposing it looked, and the more fanciful her plan along with it.

She must be crazy.

It would never work.

He'd just stepped out of the shower when the buzzer to his apartment sounded. He growled as he lashed a towel around his hips, wondering what his mother had forgotten, but no, Isobel was not the sort to give advance warning, not since he'd once lent her the key she'd made a habit of forgetting to return.

So he chose to ignore it as he swiped up another towel to rub his hair. He did all his work at his city office or out at the Esquivel estate in Getaria. Nobody called on him here unless they were invited. And then the buzzer sounded again, longer this time, more insistent, clearly designed to get his attention.

And he stopped rubbing his hair and wondered. Had Bianca been waiting for his return, keeping a safe distance from his mother? She had known his travel plans. She'd known he was due back today.

Serendipity, he thought, because she could hardly read anything into one last night if she'd invited herself back. Why not enjoy one last night together for old time's sake? And tomorrow or the next day, for that matter, he could tell her that her services were no longer required.

'Bianca, *hola,*' he said into the intercom, feeling a kick of interest from beneath his towel and thinking it fortuitous he wouldn't have to waste any time getting undressed.

His greeting met with silence until, 'It's not Bianca,' someone said in faltering Spanish, her husky voice tripping over her words and making a mess of what she was trying to say. 'It's Simone Hamilton, Felipe Otxoa's granddaughter.'

He didn't respond for a moment, his mind trying to join the dots. Did he even know Felipe had a granddaughter? They might be neighbours but it wasn't as if they were friends. But no—he rubbed his brow—there was something he remembered—a daughter who had married an Australian—the one who had been killed in some kind of accident some months back. Was this their daughter, then? It could explain why she was murdering his language. 'What do you want?' he asked in English.

'Please, Señor Esquivel,' she said, and he could almost hear her sigh of relief as the words poured out, 'I need to speak to you. It's about Felipe.'

'What about Felipe?'

'Can I come up?'

'Not until you tell me what this is about. What's so important that you have to come to my apartment?'

'Felipe, he's… Well, he's dying.'

He blinked. He'd heard talk at the estate that the old man wasn't well. He wasn't unmoved but Felipe was old and he hadn't exactly been surprised at the news. He still didn't see what it had to do with him.

'I'm sorry to hear that, but what do you expect me to do about it?'

He heard noises around her, of a family back fresh from the beach, the children being scolded by their mother for tracking sand back to one of the lower apartments, a father, grunting and grumpy and wearying of his so-called holiday and probably already dreaming about a return to the office. She tried to say something then, her words drowned out by the racket before she sighed and spoke louder. 'Can I please come up and explain? It's a bit awkward trying to discuss it like this.'

'I'm still not sure what I can do for you.'

'Please. I won't stay long. But it's important.'

Maybe to her. As far as he was concerned, Felipe had been a cantankerous old man for as long as he could remember and, whatever the distant reason for the feud between their two families, Felipe had done nothing to build any bridges over the intervening decades. But then, neither had his father during his lifetime. In a way it was a shame he hadn't been alive the day some lucky gambler had knocked on Alesander's door and offered him the acres of vines he'd won from Felipe in a game of cards. His father had been trying to buy the old man out for years.

He raked his fingers through his hair. The vines. That must be why the granddaughter was here. Had Felipe sent this hesitant little mouse with some sob story to plead for their return? He would have known he'd get short shrift if he tried such a tactic himself.

Maybe he should let her in long enough to tell her exactly that. He glanced down at his towel. Although now was hardly the time. 'I'm not actually dressed for visitors. Call me at my office.'

'My grandfather is dying, Señor Esquivel,' she said before he cut the connection. 'Do you really think I care what you are wearing?' And the hesitant mouse with the husky drawl sounded as if she'd found a backbone, and suddenly his interest was piqued. Why not humour his neighbour's granddaughter with five minutes of his time? It wasn't as if it was going to cost him anything and it would give him a chance to see if the rest of her lived up to that husky voice.

'In that case,' he said, smiling to himself as he pressed the lift release, 'you'd better come right up.'

Simone's heart lurched as the lift door opened to the small lobby that marked the entrance to the top floor apartment, her mind still reeling with the unexpected success of making it this far, her senses still reeling from the sound of Alesander's voice. Her research might have turned up his address and told her that Alesander Esquivel was San Sebastian's most eligible bachelor, but it hadn't warned her about his richly accented voice, or the way it could curl down the phone line and bury itself deep into her senses.

Yet even with that potent distraction, she'd somehow managed to keep her nerve and win an audience with the only man who could help her right now.

Alesander Esquivel, good-looking heir to the Esquivel fortune, according to her research, but then how he looked or how big his fortune was irrelevant. She was far more interested in the fact he was unmarried.

Thirty-two years old, with no wife and no fiancée, and he'd agreed to see her.

She dragged in air. It was a good start. Now all

she had to do was get him to listen long enough to consider her plan.

'Piece of cake,' she whispered to herself, in blatant denial of the dampness of her palms as she swiped them on her skirt. And then there was nothing else for it but to press on the apartment's buzzer and try to smile.

A smile that was whisked away, along with the door, somewhere between two snowy towels, one hooked around his neck, stark white against his black hair and golden skin, the other one lashed low over his hips.

Dangerously low.

She swallowed.

Thought about leaving.

Thought about staying.

Thought about that towel and whether he was wearing anything underneath it and immediately wished she hadn't.

'Simone Hamilton, I presume,' he said, and his delicious Spanish accent turned her name into a caress. She blinked and forced her eyes higher, up past that tightly ridged belly and sculpted chest, forcing them not to linger when it was all they craved to do. 'It is a pleasure to meet you.'

His dark eyes were smiling down at her, the lips on his wide mouth turned up at the corners, while the full force of the accent that had curled so evocatively down the telephone line to her now seemed to stroke the very skin under her clothes. She shivered a little as her breasts firmed, her nipples peaking inside her thin bra and, for the first time in a long time, her thoughts turned full-frontal to sex, her mind suddenly filled with images of tangled limbs and a pillow-strewn bed and this man somewhere in the midst of it all—minus the towels…

And the pictures were so vivid and powerful that she forgot all about congratulating herself for making it this far. 'I'm disturbing you,' she managed to whisper. *I'm disturbed.* 'I should come back.'

'I warned you I wasn't dressed for visitors.' He let that sink in for just a moment. 'You said you didn't care what I was wearing.'

She nodded weakly. She did recall saying

something like that. But never for one moment had she imagined he'd be wearing nothing more than a towel. She swallowed. 'But you're not… I mean… Maybe another time.'

His smile widened and her discomfort level ratcheted up with every tweak of his lips. He was enjoying himself. At her expense. 'You said it was important. Something about Felipe?'

She blinked up at him and remembered why she was here. Remembered what she was about to propose and all the reasons it would never work. Added new reasons to the list—because the pictures she'd found hadn't done him justice—he wasn't just another good—looking man with a nice body, he was a veritable god-and because men who looked like gods married super-models and heiresses and princesses and not women who rocked up on their doorstep asking for favours.

And because nobody in their right mind would ever believe a man like him would hook up with a woman like her.

Oh God, what was she even doing here?

'I'm sorry,' she said, shaking her head. 'Coming here was a mistake.' She was halfway to turning but he had hold of her forearm and, before she knew it, she was propelled inside his apartment with the promise of fresh coffee on his lips and the door closed firmly behind her.

'Sit down,' he ordered, gesturing towards a leather sofa twice the length of her flat at home and yet dwarfed here by the sheer dimensions of the long, high-ceilinged room that seemed to let the whole of the bay in through one expansive wall of glass. 'Maybe now you could tell me what this is all about.'

She sat obediently, absently rubbing her arm where he'd touched her, the skin still tingling as if his touch had set nerve endings dancing under her skin. But then, why wouldn't she be nervy when she didn't know which way to look to avoid staring at his masculine perfection; when every time her eyes did stray too close to his toned, bronzed body, they wanted to lock and hold and drink him in?

How could she even start to explain when she

didn't know where to look and when her tongue seemed suddenly twice its size?

'All right,' she said, 'if you insist. But I'll give you a minute to get dressed first.'

'No rush,' he said, dashing her hopes of any relief while he poured coffee from a freshly brewed jug. He didn't ask her how she wanted it or even if she wanted it, simply stirred in sugar and milk and handed it to her. She took it, careful to fix her gaze on the cup, equally careful to avoid brushing her fingers with his and all the while wondering why she'd ever been crazy enough to think this might work. 'So tell me, what's wrong with Felipe?' he asked, reminding her again of the reason why she was here, and she wondered at his ability to make her forget what should be foremost in her mind.

Giving Felipe a reason to smile.

She'd made it this far. She owed it to Felipe to follow through. She'd return to Melbourne one day after all. The humiliation wouldn't last for ever...

So much for wondering if she matched her

husky voice. Instead she looked like a waif, he thought, lost and lonely, her grey-blue eyes too big and her mouth almost too wide for her thin heart-shaped face, while her cotton shirt bagged around her lean frame. She stared blankly at the cup in her hands, whatever fight she'd called upon to secure this interview seemingly gone. She looked tiny against the sofa. Exactly like that mouse he'd imagined her to be when she'd first spoken so hesitantly on the phone.

'You said he was dying,' he prompted. And suddenly her chin kicked up and she found that husky note that had captured his interest earlier.

'The doctor said he has six months to live. Maybe twelve.' Her voice cracked a little on the twelve and she put the cup in her hands down before she recovered enough to continue, 'I don't think he'll last that long.'

She pushed honey-blonde hair that had fallen free from her ponytail behind her ears before she looked up at him, her eyes glassy and hollow. 'I'm sorry,' she said, swiping a rogue tear from her cheek. 'I've made a complete mess of this. You didn't need this.'

He didn't, but that didn't mean he wasn't a little bit curious about why she thought it so necessary to knock on his door to ask for his help. He had his suspicions, of course—but he had to admit that the whole granddaughter turning up on his doorstep to plead her case was unexpected. 'Why do you think Felipe won't last that long?'

She shrugged almost impatiently, as if the reason was blindingly obvious and there was nothing else it could be. 'Because he's given up. He thinks he deserves to die.'

'Because of the land?'

'Of course, because of the land! It's about losing his wife and daughter too, but don't you see, losing the land on top of everything else is killing him faster than any disease.'

'I knew it.' He padded barefoot to the window, strangely disappointed, regretting the impulse to let her in, and not only because his curiosity about Felipe's long lost granddaughter with the husky drawl had been satisfied with one look at this skinny, big-eyed waif. But because he'd been right. Of course it had to be about the land. And yet for some reason being right gave him no pleasure.

Maybe because he knew what would come next, and that any moment now she'd be asking for the favour she'd obviously come here to ask—for him to either return the land out of the goodness of his heart, or to lend her the money to buy it back.

He should never have let her in. Felipe should never have sent her. What had the old man been thinking, to send her to plead his case? Had he been hoping he'd feel sorry for her and agree to whatever she asked? A coiling anger unfurled inside him that anyone, let alone his father's old nemesis, would think him so easily manipulated.

'So that's why he sent you, then? To ask for it back?'

Maybe his words sounded more like accusations than questions, maybe he sounded more combative than inquisitive, because she flinched, her face tight, her eyes clearly on the defensive. 'Felipe didn't send me. He doesn't even know I'm here.' She hesitated before saying anything more, before she glanced at the watch on her slim wrist and looked up again, already gathering herself, her face suddenly resolute, as if she'd decided something. 'Look, maybe I should go—'

He stalled her preparations to leave with a shrivelling glare. 'You do realise it wasn't me who gambled the property out from underneath him, don't you? I bought it fair and square. And I paid a hefty premium for the privilege.'

'I know that.'

'Then surely you don't expect me to hand it calmly back, no matter how ill you say your grandfather is.'

Her blue eyes flashed icicles, her manner changing as swiftly as if someone had flicked a switch. 'Do you think I'm that stupid? I may be a stranger here, but Felipe has told me enough about the Esquivels to know that would never happen.'

He bristled at her emphasis on the word 'never'.

It was true, Felipe and his father had had their differences in the past, and yes, the Esquivels took their business seriously, but that did not mean they did not act without honour. They were Basques after all. 'Then why did you come? Is it money you want?'

She gave a toss of her head, setting her ponytail lurching from side to side, the ends she'd poked behind her ears swinging free once more. 'I don't want your money. I don't care about your money.'

'So why are you here? What other reason could you possibly have for turning up on my doorstep demanding a private hearing?'

She stood up then, all five feet nothing of her, but with her dark eyes flashing, her jaw set in a flushed face and an attitude that spoke more of bottled rage than the meek little mouse who had turned up on his doorstep.

'All right. Since you really want to know, I came here to ask if you would marry me.'

CHAPTER THREE

'MARRY YOU?' HE didn't wait for her to say any more. He'd heard enough. He laughed out loud, the sound reverberating around the room. He'd known she'd wanted something—land or money—and she had wanted something, but a proposal of marriage had never been on his radar. 'You're seriously proposing marriage?'

'I know.' His visitor clenched and unclenched her hands by her sides, her eyes frosty and hard with anger, her features set as if she didn't hold it all together, she would explode. 'Crazy idea. Forget I said anything. Clearly I was wrong to think you might lift so much as a finger to help my grandfather. Sorry to bother you. I'll see myself out.'

She wheeled around, her skirt flaring high as she spun to reveal legs more shapely than he would have imagined she possessed before they marched her purposefully towards the door, her words rankling more with each stride. How dare she come out with a crazy proposal like that and then make out that he'd let her down?

He caught up with her as she pulled the door open, slamming it shut the next second with the flat of his hand over her shoulder. 'I don't remember you asking me to lift a finger.' She wasn't listening. Either that or she simply took no notice. She worked the handle frantically with both hands, her slim body straining as she pulled with all her might, while the door refused to budge so much as an inch with his weight to keep it closed.

'Let me out!'

He stayed right where he was, with the tiny fury beneath him working away on the door, bracing herself against the wall for leverage. 'On the other hand, I do recall you asking me to marry you.'

'It was a mistake,' she said, frantic and half breathless from her efforts.

'What, you mean you meant to ask someone else?'

She gave up on the handle, staring at the door as if willing it to disappear with the sheer force of her will. 'I thought you might help. Turns out I was wrong.'

'And so now you make out that I've somehow let you down? Because I'm honest and laugh when you suggest something as ridiculous as marrying you?'

'Ridiculous because you're such a catch, you mean? God, you're unbelievable! Do you actually believe I *want* to marry you?'

She gave the door a final kick and spun around and almost immediately wished she hadn't, suddenly confronted by the naked wall of his chest just inches from her face. Bronzed olive skin roughened with dark hair and two hard nipples jutting out at her. God, why the hell couldn't the man just put on some clothes? Because this close she could see his chest hair sway in the breeze from her breath. This close she could smell the lemon soap he'd used while bathing; could smell the clean scent of masculine skin.

And she really didn't need to know that she liked the combination.

'You tell me,' he answered roughly. 'You're the one doing the asking.'

He had her boxed in on two sides, one arm planted beside her head, the door at her back, with only one avenue of escape left to her. Tempting as it was, she got the distinct impression this man would love it if she tried to flee again. He would no doubt feed off the thrill. So she stayed exactly where she was and forced her eyes higher to meet his.

'A few months,' she said. 'I wasn't asking for forever. I'm not that much of a masochist.'

Something flickered in his eyes as he leaned dangerously down over her, and she wondered at the logic of throwing insults at the only man who could help her. Though that had been before he'd laughed her proposal down without even bothering to listen to her. Now there was obviously nothing to gain by being polite—and nothing to lose by telling him exactly how little she wanted this for herself. 'If there was any other way, believe me, I'd grab it with both hands.'

His dark eyes searched hers, his chin set, the tendons on his neck standing out in thick cords. 'What kind of game are you playing? Why are you really here?'

She might have told him if she thought he might actually listen. 'Look, there's no point going on with this. Let me go now and I promise never to darken your door again. Maybe there's even a slight chance we might forget this unfortunate event ever took place.'

'Forget a scrawny slip of a girl I've never met asking me to marry her? Forget a proposal of marriage that comes dressed in barbs and insults from a woman who, by her own admission, wishes there was some other way? I don't think I'm going to forget that in a hurry. Not when she hasn't even explained why.'

'Is there any point? I'd say you made your position crystal clear. Obviously there's no way you'd lower yourself to marry "a scrawny slip of a girl".'

Her eyes flashed cold fire as she spat his words back at him, anger mixed with hurt. She was smarting at his insult, he could tell, and maybe she had a point. Maybe she was more petite than scrawny, though it was hard to tell, her body buried under a chain-store cotton skirt and top that left everything to the imagination. But she was no mere girl. Because, from his vantage point above her he could see the slight swell of her breasts as her chest rose and fell. This close he could see her eyes were more blue than grey, the colour of early morning sky before the sun burned away the mist from the hillsides. And this close he could smell her scent, a mix of honey and sunshine and feminine awareness, the unmistakable scent of a woman who was turned on.

His body responded the only way it knew how, surprising him, because she was nothing like his usual type of woman and he wasn't interested. If he had been interested he would have known it the moment he'd opened the door and laid eyes on her, the way it usually worked.

And once again he regretted the sudden absence of Bianca. Clearly it had been too long if he was getting horny over any random big-eyed waif who turned up on his doorstep. He willed the growing stiffness away, his decision not to put any clothes on intended more to amuse himself rather than any attempt at seduction. And then his eyes drifted down again, lingering over the spot where the neckline gaped, exposing skin that looked like satin.

Admittedly a big-eyed waif with unexpected curves…

'Then again, maybe not so scrawny,' he said, unable to resist putting a hand to her shoulder in spite of the fact he wasn't really interested, his thumb testing the texture of her skin, finding it as smooth as his vision had promised.

She shivered under his touch, her blue eyes wide, her bottom lip trembling, right before she shot away sideways. 'Don't touch me!'

He turned, amused by his unexpected visitor

and her propensity to move from flight to fight and back again in a heartbeat. 'What is this? You ask me to marry you and then say I can't touch? Surely you must have come prepared for an audition.'

She wrapped her arms tightly around her waist. 'No! There will be no audition! The marriage is for Felipe. Only for Felipe.' Outside the windows the light was starting to fade, the afternoon sun slipping away, while inside her cheeks were lit up, her eyes flashed cold blue flame and her hands were balled in fists so tight that, unlike the rest of her, her knuckles showed white. 'Haven't you got a robe or something?'

He smiled at the sudden change in topic, holding his arms out by his sides innocently. 'Do you have a problem with what I'm wearing?'

'That's just it. You're not really wearing anything.' She paused suddenly, biting her lip, almost as if she'd said too much and revealed too much of herself in the process. Then she hastily added, 'I'd hate for you to catch cold or something.'

As if that was her reason. His amusement was growing by the minute, his visitor unexpectedly entertaining. It wasn't just because the idea was so crazy he wondered how this woman, who seemed more timid than tigress despite her attempts, had found the courage to carry it off, but maybe because his mother had been here not an hour ago berating him on his reluctance to find a wife. He half wished she'd been here to witness this. Though no doubt she would be more appalled than amused, but then, that thought only amused him even more.

'Then you will be relieved to know I have a very healthy constitution,' he said, 'but the last thing I wish is for you to feel uncomfortable.' He excused himself for a moment to pull on fresh clothes, though not so much for her comfort level but because it suited him to do so. He'd had his sport and the last thing he wanted was for her to think he was interested in her sexually. He was intrigued, it was true, and now that the shock of her surprise proposal was over, he was curious to hear more, but there was no point encouraging her.

* * *

She was still here. Simone let out a breath she hadn't realised she'd been holding and turned to gaze out of the windows over the million euro view. He hadn't thrown her out and neither had he let her flee. She was still here and he was going to cover himself up.

Surely that counted as success on two counts?

And now, for whatever reason, he actually seemed willing to listen to her.

Even better, maybe once he had covered up that chest and all that toned olive-gold skin, she might even be able to think straight. She could only hope. Being forced to look at all that masculine perfection without actually looking like she was looking at it was one hell of a distraction otherwise. When he'd had her backed against the door and touched his fingers to her shoulder, she'd felt the sizzle shoot straight to her core. Although maybe it was the hungry look in his eyes that had turned his touch electric…

God, what must it be like to be a woman who actually wanted him to touch her? She shivered, her body remembering the electric thrill. Dangerous, she thought, definitely dangerous. Thank God she wasn't going there.

'I apologise for keeping you waiting.'

His richly accented voice stroked its way down her spine, almost convincing her that he meant every word he said. She turned to find him dressed not in a robe, as she'd been half-expecting, but in light-coloured trousers and a fine knitted top that skimmed over the wall of his chest in a way she really didn't want to think too much about. So she pushed her wayward hair behind her ears and looked elsewhere and found his feet instead. 'Nice shoes,' she said lamely, for want of anything better to say.

He glanced down at his leather loafers. 'I have a man who makes them for me. He is very good.'

Handmade shoes, she pondered, really studying them this time, wishing she could hide away her own scuffed ballet flats. She'd known he had money, sure, but what was this world she'd dared enter, a world where he probably spent more on a pair of shoes than she had on her entire wardrobe? And it wasn't as if he wouldn't know that. It was a wonder he hadn't let her flee while he'd had the chance. It was a wonder he hadn't slammed the door in her face.

'But you didn't come here to compliment me on my footwear,' he prompted, gesturing towards a sofa as he sprawled himself into a wide armchair, 'I am curious to hear more—a marriage between you and me, but for Felipe? How does that work, exactly?'

She lowered herself down tentatively on the edge of the sofa, her heart racing with the possibilities. He wanted to hear more. Was he was simply curious, as he claimed, or was he actually entertaining her proposal? 'You really want to know? You won't laugh this time?'

'You took me by surprise,' he admitted with a shrug. 'It is not everyday a woman asks me to marry her while at the same time claiming she would rather be torn apart by wild horses or eaten by sharks.'

She pressed her lips together, not bothering to deny she'd used those words, knowing he was poking fun at her and yet thoroughly discon-

certed by his smile. He was good-looking even
when he was angry, the strong lines of his face
too well put together to be distorted by rage, but
when he smiled he was absolutely devastating.
'I'm sorry. It's not every day that I ask a man to
marry me.'

He nodded. 'I'm flattered,' he said, sounding
anything but. 'So tell me, what is this marriage
all about? Why is it so necessary, you believe,
to marry me? What are you trying to achieve?'

'I want to make Felipe's last days happy.'

'You think you will make him happy by marrying the son of a man he was in dispute with
almost his entire life?'

'I believe it will make him happy to believe
his vineyard is reunited.' And when she saw her
words made no impact on him, she continued,
more passionately, this time. 'Don't you see,
those vines you bought were Felipe's life. And
right now every time he looks out of his window he's reminded of his mistake. Every time
he looks out of his window, he's reminded of
all that he lost.' She shook her head. 'And right

now he doesn't care about the remaining vines. He doesn't care about anything.' She gazed up at him, wanting to make him understand. Desperate to make him understand. 'I know it sounds mad, but if he could see a marriage between our families, he would also see the vineyard reunited, and whatever mistakes he made—well, they wouldn't matter any more. He might smile again, if he realised that all was not lost.'

'And so Felipe dies happy.'

She winced at his words and he found himself wondering if she was acting. How could she care so much about a man who must be almost a stranger to her? 'It would only be for a few months. The doctors said—'

'You told me.' He stood suddenly and wandered to the windows, his back to her. 'Six to twelve months. But why should I believe what you say? It seems to me that you have the most to gain out of this arrangement. How do I know you won't try to get pregnant and find yet another reason to "reunite" our families, this time on a more permanent basis?'

He thought her capable of doing that? God, what kind of people was he used to dealing with? She gave a tight shake of her head, feeling sick at the thought of there being any chance a pregnancy would result from this union. 'There is no chance of that. This would be purely a business arrangement. Nothing more.'

'So you say, but how can I believe you?'

'Quite easily.' She looked at him levelly, her blue-grey eyes as cold as the deepest sea. 'There will be no pregnancy because there will be no sex.'

He looked back at her over his shoulder in surprise, one eyebrow arched. 'No sex? You really think a marriage can work without sex?'

'Why not? It's not a real marriage so there's no need for sex. What I'm proposing is a marriage in name only. Besides, it's not as if we even like each other. We barely even know each other, for that matter. Why would we need or even want to have sex?'

He shrugged aside every one of her objections as irrelevant. He'd never actually considered whether he actually liked someone as a barrier to having sex with them. Then again, from what he could ascertain, his father hadn't slept with his mother for the last thirty years of their marriage, which proved marriage without sex between husband and wife was possible, even if his father hadn't gone without, by all accounts.

Which was probably a point worth making...

'If I agreed to this marriage,' he said, pausing when he noticed the sudden flare in her eyes and wanting to damp it down before she got too excited, 'that's *if* I agree, and I agreed to your condition of a marriage in name only, you do understand that there will be other women? That I would need to have sex with someone.'

Her lips tightened. Her entire posture tightened. 'I'm sure you have no shortage of friends and acquaintances who would be only too happy to accommodate your needs. I wouldn't stand in your way, so long as you were discreet, of course.'

He stroked his chin thoughtfully and her eyes were drawn again to the strong lines of his face, the dramatic planes and dark-as-night eyes and wished his features weren't anywhere near as well put together. 'Then possibly it might work,' he said, 'And possibly you are also right about not having sex. It's not as if you're my type, after all.'

'Fine!' she snapped, her eyes wide, her cheeks flaring with colour. 'So much the better!'

'*Bueno,*' he said, smiling at her snippy response because, for her all her eagerness to announce that she had no interest in having sex with him, it was clear she didn't want to hear the reasons why he might not be interested in having sex with her. 'So long as we understand each other. As you've mentioned, we don't know how long such a marriage might last. Several months. A year. You couldn't expect me to remain celibate for the duration.'

'I would hate you to have to suppress your natural desires, although perhaps you might try exercising just a little more control.'

'Why should I? I like sex.'

'I don't want to hear it! All I know is that if

you agree to this, there will be no sex between us. So there will be no chance of a child. So there can be no "complications".'

He sighed as he turned back towards the window, the light fading from the sky, the lighting around the Bay coming on, turning the shoreline to gold. Perhaps she was right. Without sex there could be no unwanted pregnancy. No complications, just as she said. Which meant no chance for her to claim against the Esquivel estate.

And meanwhile this marriage would get his mother off his back into the deal.

He almost laughed. There would be no point in Ezmerelda continuing to wait for him to propose because he'd already be married. It was utterly delicious. He couldn't remember when he'd ever been tempted by such a crazy deal. But would anyone believe it? Would anyone actually believe that, of all the women in the world, he had chosen this particular one to marry? Because he hadn't been joking. She was nothing like his usual kind of woman. He preferred his woman more overtly sexual, whereas this woman looked like a waif in her baggy clothes.

And even though there was something about her cool blue eyes and her husky voice, and there was something of feminine shape hidden away that he'd caught a glimpse of, if he was to agree to anything, the terms would definitely need some work. He would need a bit more of an incentive if he was going to bother to make their arrangement look convincing.

'It's very noble of you, sacrificing yourself on the altar of marriage for your grandfather's benefit. But why should I go along with it? What would be in it for me, given you've ruled out sex?'

She blinked up at him and he could tell she was completely unprepared for the question. He wondered at her naivety. Did she imagine he would go along with this out of the goodness of his heart? 'Well,' she began, 'you do now have most of Felipe's vineyard.'

'I told you, I bought that land, fair and square. That land is mine already.'

'But you knew how he'd lost it. You took advantage of an old man's misfortune because it suited you.'

'If I hadn't bought it, someone else would have.'

'But *you're* the one who bought it and don't tell me you didn't jump at the chance. Felipe told me your father had been trying to get him off his land for decades.'

'And you think that my agreeing to this will ease my conscience over the fact a large chunk of his estate is now mine?' He shook his head. 'No, my conscience is clear. I don't have any trouble sleeping at night. In which case, you're offering me nothing. And if I'm going to agree to this, I need a real incentive.'

Her heart jumped in her chest. *'If I'm going to agree to this'?* Was he serious? Was she that close to getting him to agree to her crazy plan? She licked her lips. 'So what would it take to secure your agreement?' she asked tentatively, almost afraid to breathe as she waited for his response.

'Am I right in thinking Felipe will leave the balance of the estate to you, as his sole beneficiary?'

She blinked. 'Um, yes, he still has to see a lawyer to change his will, but he's mentioned that's what he wants to do.'

'Then that's my price. When Felipe dies and you inherit, I want you to agree that you'll sign over the rest of the estate to me.'

'All of it?'

'There's not a whole lot left—and you do want me to marry you, don't you, so Felipe believes his precious vines are reunited once more?'

'Of course I do.'

'Then, subject to your final agreement of my terms, I'd say that makes us officially engaged.'

CHAPTER FOUR

'WHAT'S IT TO BE, my prospective wife? You decide. Do we have a deal?'

Did they? Her heart was hammering so loud she could scarcely hear herself think. Half of her was already celebrating. She'd done the unthinkable and secured Alesander's agreement. Soon Felipe would see his precious vines reunited under the mantle of their marriage.

But after he was gone—after their marriage was dissolved—they would stay reunited. Alesander would own the entire estate.

He was waiting for her answer, his half-smile telling her that he was already anticipating her agreement.

Should she accept his terms?

Felipe had promised her what was left of the estate when he died, wanting the vines to stay in the family, wanting to ensure that she would be taken care of financially. After her spendthrift parents had left her with nothing but a few trinkets, it would have been all that she owned. And now, if she agreed to Alesander's terms, she'd be left with nothing again.

But what good were the vines to her anyway when her plan had always been to return to her studies in Melbourne? What point was there in her keeping them, other than as a link to a past and a life she'd been denied most of her life? She didn't belong here. Not really. She was no vigneron, whatever her heritage. She couldn't even speak the language. Not properly. 'All right,' she said, her voice little more than a whisper, knowing that ultimately she had no choice. 'You have a deal.'

'Good, I'll get my lawyers to draft up the agreement.'

'This can't get out! Felipe must not suspect.'

'You think I want it to become public knowledge? No, my legal people will not breathe a word of this. Nobody will know our marriage is not real.'

She nodded, feeling her shoulders sag and her very bones droop, suddenly bone-weary. She'd come here and achieved what she'd never thought she'd achieve—the impossible had happened and Alesander Esquivel had agreed to her crazy plan. Soon the vineyard would be reunited and Felipe would have a reason to smile again. She should be over the moon ecstatic right now. And yet instead she felt wrung out, both emotionally and physically. 'I must go,' she said, shocked when she glanced out of the window and realised how the light was fading from the day. 'Felipe will be wondering where I am.' She looked back at him. 'I imagine you'll be in touch when the papers are ready to sign.'

'I'll get my jacket. I'll drive you home.'

'There's no need,' she said, even as he was disappearing into his room. She would be fine on the local bus. She would be even later home but she could do with the time to think. And right now she could do with the space to breathe air not spiced with this man's scent, a blend of citrus, musk and one hundred per cent testosterone.

'There's every need,' he said, returning with a jacket he shrugged over his shoulders, a set of keys in his hand. 'There are things we need to discuss.'

'Like what?'

'Like how we met, for a start. We need to get our stories straight and I'm assuming you'd prefer I didn't go around telling people you knocked on my door and asked me to marry you. Plus we need to work out how quickly to progress this arrangement. Given the state of Felipe's health, I'm guessing you're not after a long engagement?'

'Well, no...' She hadn't really thought about it. He was right, of course, it was just that she hadn't given herself the luxury of thinking that far ahead. Not when she'd never actually been confident of pulling this plan off and securing his agreement.

'Then let's make it next month—it'll take that long for the legalities, and meanwhile we need to be seen together and in the right places. We can work that out on the way.' He snatched up car keys from a drawer. 'Besides, I think it's about time I reacquainted myself with my prospective grandfather-in-law.'

His car was low and lean and looked more as if it belonged on a racetrack than on any road. It didn't help that it was black. She regarded it suspiciously. 'Are you sure this is street legal?'

He laughed, a low rumbling laugh that she felt uncomfortably low in her belly, as he ushered her into the low-slung GTA Spano that seemed filled with leather and aluminium and cool LCD lighting.

Safe in her leather seat, the car wrapped around her like an embrace, the panoramic glass roof bringing the outside inside.

He didn't so much drive through the busy streets of San Sebastian as prowled, driver and machine like a predator, waiting for just the right moment to switch lanes or to overtake, using the vehicle's cat-like manoeuvrability and power to masterfully take control of the streets, until they hit the highway and the car changed gears and ate up the few miles before the turn-off to the coast and small fishing village of Getaria.

Along the way they sorted the story of how they'd met by chance in San Sebastian when she'd stopped him on the street to ask directions. Or rather, Alesander sorted their story, while she tried hard to ignore the blood-dizzying effect of sharing the same confined space with him. She didn't have to turn her head and see him to know he was right there beside her, she could taste him in the very air she breathed, and somehow the scent of leather only added to the heady mix. She didn't have to watch his long-fingered hands to know when they were on the steering wheel or when he changed gears because she could feel the whisper of air that stirred against her leg.

It was disconcerting. She couldn't remember when she'd ever been so aware of anyone in her entire life.

Or especially any man.

But then she'd never asked anyone else to marry her before either, much less have them agree. This was brand new territory for her. Little wonder she was so on edge.

The closer they got to Getaria, the more anxious she grew and she found herself wishing she'd caught the bus after all. Now she'd have no chance to warn Felipe that she'd bumped into Alesander, no chance to let him get used to the idea before having him turn up on the doorstep. He would come around, she was sure, but he was bound to be a little unreceptive at first.

'Don't be surprised if Felipe is a little gruff towards you,' she warned. 'Given what's happened, I mean.'

'Given the fact I own three-quarters of his estate now, you mean?' He shrugged. 'As long as I have been alive and, indeed, for a long time before, things have never been easy between our two families.'

'Why is that? What happened?'

'What is the reason behind any family rivalry? A cross word. A dark look. And, in this case, a bride stolen out from under my great-great-grandfather's nose and married to another before he could stop her.'

'Who did she marry?'

'Felipe's grandfather.'

'Oh, I see. Wow.' She shook her head. 'But still, that must have happened years ago. Surely something that happened a century ago isn't still a sore point. The families are neighbours after all.'

'Honour is very important to the Basque people and memories are long. One does not forget when one's pride has been trampled upon.'

'I guess not.' And she wondered how she would be remembered when she was gone, after probably the shortest marriage in Esquivel history. It would, no doubt, add cause to keep resentment towards the Otxoa name simmering for the next century or more. Just as well she could disappear home to Australia when the marriage was dissolved. 'What about your family? How will they take the news of you marrying an Otxoa?'

He smiled. 'Not well. At least not initially. But I will tell them it is time to move on. I will make them come around and see that we cannot hold a grudge between our families for ever. And then, when it is over, they will delight in telling me that they told me so and that they were right all along.'

'Will you mind that?'

'I don't care what anyone says, not when I'm going to end up with the land.'

'Oh, of course,' she said. The land that made it all worthwhile. *The land she'd bargained away.* His family would probably forgive him anything for that.

'Tell me,' he said, changing the topic, 'is there a boyfriend at home in Australia waiting for you to return home? Who might be upset about your getting married and turn up suddenly to stop the wedding?'

She laughed. She couldn't help it, the thought of Damon turning up to claim her from the clutches of marriage to another man too funny not to laugh out loud. But Damon wouldn't have the guts to show his face, even if he had decided he wanted to get back with her. 'No. No boy-friend.'

He looked across at her. 'You make it sound like there was one.'

'There was, for a while. But he's history and he's staying there. Believe me, he won't be turning up to stop the wedding.'

'What about other friends or family? Won't they be concerned for you?'

'There's no family to speak of. Not now.'

'But your father's family?'

She shook her head. 'I know it sounds odd, but I never met them. Dad discovered he was adopted when he was thirteen and he never forgave his adoptive family for keeping the secret from him for so long. And he never met his birth parents but he hated them for abandoning him in the first place. I think that's why he and Mum got on so well together. They understood each other. They were alone in the world and they were all each other had.'

'Surely they had you?'

'They did but…' She raised her head, searching the night sky through the clear glass roof for the words. How did one go about explaining such personal things to someone who was a virtual stranger, and yet who should not be such a stranger, given they were now engaged to be married? How much did he need to know? How much did she need to tell him?

And yet there was something liberating, too, about sharing something about your family with a total stranger, knowing that it would never matter. After all, it wasn't as if he'd ever have to meet her parents. Not now.

'I always thought Mum was all Dad ever wanted or needed.'

He looked her way and she caught his frown.

'Don't get me wrong, he was a good dad, sometimes great,' she said wistfully, remembering a particular father and daughter three-legged race on the one primary school sports day. They'd come last but it didn't matter, because at least that year he'd actually bothered to turn up, despite the fact he'd never had a job to go to like the other dads and had always made excuses and she'd spent every year watching her friends run with their fathers. But he'd turned up that year and she'd been beside herself, bursting with pride.

He'd done it for her, she'd realised years later, because she'd pleaded for the weeks and days before with him to go, and finally she'd worn him down, but at the time it had felt like Christmas.

'Really, it was okay. I just got the impression he would have been perfectly happy never having kids. I guess I always just felt a little surplus to requirements.'

'You have no other family? No brothers or sisters?'

'No.'

He didn't reply and she didn't mind because she was more than content to look out of the window, looking at the rows of vines trellised so high above the hillside that you could walk beneath them, so different to the style of vineyard she was used to seeing at home. And it was easier for a moment to think about the tangle of vines than the tangle of families.

For a moment. Until she remembered another tangling thread.

'Dad didn't want Mum to come back to Spain, you know, when she heard that her mother was dying. He didn't want her to rebuild any bridges and reconnect with a father he said had abandoned her. In all honesty, I think he only let her come in the end because he figured Felipe was old and it might result in an inheritance that might pay off their debts.

'What he didn't figure on was Mum and Felipe actually getting on okay. He expected they'd pick up where they'd left off last time and they'd shout the house down, but this time was different, I think because her mother had died. And Mum had grown up a bit and Felipe had mellowed and both she and Felipe were starting to realise all the things they'd missed.'

'He must have been happy to have you around, after losing Maria.'

He shouldn't have had to wait that long. She clamped down on a boulder of guilt she'd felt, heavy and weighted inside her from the day she'd heard Maria had died. Sometimes she could lock it away and almost forget it was there, and other times it would escape and roll awkwardly through her gut, crushing her spirit and making her remember a promise that she'd made to herself so many years ago.

A promise she'd broken.

She dragged in air. But she was here now. It wasn't too late to make things better; to make up just a little bit for all that had gone before.

'He was. We all were, all apart from Dad. He resented Mum talking in a language and laughing at jokes he couldn't understand.' Tears once again stung her eyes and she clamped down on the urge to cry. He was her father and she'd loved him but there were times she'd wanted to shake him too, and make him see that he didn't have to take on the whole world to enjoy it. 'And now they've both gone and Felipe is dying too.' She turned her head away as two fat tears squeezed their way from the corners of her eyes, swiping the wetness from her cheeks.

'The last few months have been rough on you.'

She squeezed damp eyes shut, wishing away the sting, trying to block out his rich, low voice from worming its way into anywhere it could do some damage. She wished to hell he didn't sound so…*understanding*. She wasn't looking for sympathy. She was looking for a solution. 'Anyway,' she said, huffing out air, shaking off her gloom, 'I'm not planning on telling anyone at home about this—about our arrangement. Nobody need know. Because then I don't have to go home and explain what went wrong with my quickie marriage. It might not bother you, but there's no way I want to listen to everyone telling me, "I told you so".'

'You'll have nobody? Don't you think it will look strange if you have no one in attendance? Isn't there a friend you can confide in and trust?'

That earned him a snort. She'd had a best friend she'd trusted. Ever since primary school, she and Carla had day-dreamed about the day they'd each get married and had sworn to be each other's chief bridesmaids. They'd shared everything in life—the good times and the bad—and the job had always been Carla's—right up until the day Simone had found her sharing her cheating boyfriend.

And not only sharing her boyfriend but sharing him in her bed, which, to her way of thinking, made the betrayal even more damning.

As for asking any of her other friends—there was no way she could expect photos or news of the wedding not to leak out onto social media, no matter how much she wanted to keep it quiet. And it would be unfair and unreasonable to ask her friends to keep it a secret, simply to protect her own need for privacy. They'd want to know why and they'd deserve to be told.

And that wouldn't work when she didn't want anyone to know. This marriage was hardly going to be one of her finest moments. She wasn't sure she wanted witnesses to the event. 'I don't know,' she said, thinking it was all getting too difficult. 'Maybe we should just fly off to Las Vegas and not bother with a wedding here at all. Just come back and say it's a done deal.'

'And cheat Felipe out of the pleasure of walking his granddaughter down the aisle? How would it brighten his days to know you had been whisked away to marry a man whose family he has been in dispute with his entire life?' He hesitated a moment to let that sink in, and sink in it did. As much as the idea appealed, how could she do that when this was all about convincing him this was real and making him happy?

'Besides,' Alesander continued, 'why should anyone believe it? Whereas if they see us married before their eyes, surely that will be more convincing.'

Convincing. What did that mean in Spanish terms? She looked out of the window, biting her lip as the car wended its way along the narrow road up the hill towards Felipe's shrunken estate. Her plan had seemed so easy when she'd come up with it. Marry Alesander and let Felipe end his days thinking his precious vines were reunited. What could be more simple?

But there was so much she hadn't considered; so many details where her plans could come unstuck.

Convincing.

But she didn't want a big church wedding with all the trimmings. Somehow a small civil affair seemed easier to undo. Less false, if there even was a scale of falseness.

Right now she wanted to believe it.

But maybe she'd been kidding herself all along. Maybe her idea had been doomed from the start and she was finally starting to realise it.

Except he must believe it was possible or why would he have gone along with it?

She turned to him, needing to hear what he thought. 'Do you really think we can make this work?'

He looked over at her. 'Having second thoughts?'

'No, not really. It's just that…it seemed like such a simple idea but there's just so much to consider. So many tiny details to sort out.'

'Ideas are the easy part. It's making them happen that takes work.'

Wasn't that the truth? 'So you think we can do it?'

'I'm banking on it.'

The land, she thought, sitting back in her seat. He will make it happen because he's banking on the land. And she couldn't resent the price he'd demanded or the deal she'd made, because right now having Alesander Esquivel on her team was her plan's biggest asset.

If she had nothing else going for her, he would make it happen.

Oh yes, Alesander thought, he was banking on it. The way he figured it, he had nothing to lose and everything to gain.

He turned the car into the driveway leading to the small estate and immediately knew that something was wrong. Very wrong. In September one expected the vines to be dense, the foliage protecting the fruit hanging in clusters beneath, but the vines either side of the driveway were overgrown and tangled, the supporting trellises broken in places so that the vines had collapsed onto the ground.

The small house at the end of the driveway had the same air of neglect.

'What is Felipe doing about the harvest? The grapes will be ready in a month or so.'

'Not a lot. Even if he cared, I don't think he'd have the strength to do much.'

'But he has people working for him, surely?'

She gave him a pointed look as she undid her seat belt and pushed open her door. 'Seriously? Does it look like he has an army of people working for him?' He wasted the time it took to curse and she was almost out of the car before he stopped her with a hand to her arm.

'Hey!'

She swung around, cold flame erupting from her blue eyes.

'I'll get those trellises fixed.'

'Whatever.' She tugged on her arm and he tightened his grip and pulled her closer.

'We're supposed to be friends, right—friends who might be a little keen on each other. So get angry with me, sure, but do it on your own time. Right now we've got a job to do.'

'A snow job, you mean.'

'Do you want this? I can leave right now if you

don't. Because I can wait a few months for this place to completely fall apart and then buy you out for a rock-bottom price if you'd prefer. Or we can do it your way. It's up to you.'

She blinked and looked up at the house, where a grizzled face craned his neck to make sense of what was going on in the driveway outside. She smiled at him and waved from inside the car before turning back to Alesander. 'Of course I do.'

'Okay, so share that smile with me, and look friendly.'

She turned on a smile so sickly-sweet she must have added a cup of saccharin to the mix. 'Thank you so much for the lift, Señor Esquivel,' she said in a voice designed not to carry, merely to convey an impression to the man sitting at the window. 'I'd like to say it's been a pleasure meeting you but that would be an out-and-out lie.'

He took her hand before she could get out and pressed the back of her hand to his mouth, loving the way her eyes threw heated sparks at the graze of his lips on her skin. 'I'm beginning to think this marriage might be more entertaining than I first thought.'

Her smile widened. She even managed a little laugh. 'Lucky you. I'm beginning to think it's going to be a real pain in the backside. Or maybe that's just you.'

'I aim to please.'

She pulled her hand free as she stepped from the car.

'Don't forget to smile,' he said behind her.

'Zer egiten ari da hemen zuen?' Felipe said from his chair near the window as she entered.

'What did you say, Abuelo?' Simone said, leaning over to give him a kiss first to one and then the other of his hollowed white-whiskered cheeks.

'He wants to know what I'm doing here.'

She nodded her thanks to Alesander behind her, and turned to invite him in. She was still angry that he could be so entirely oblivious to the contribution he'd made to Felipe's decline, but she was grateful for the translation. When her grandfather spoke in Spanish it was hard enough to keep up, but when he reverted to the regional Basque language she had no hope of understanding.

But when she looked around she had to do a double take. The room seemed to have shrunk and the modest cottage that was perfectly adequate for the two of them now seemed tiny, the roof hovering low over their visitor's head. She blinked and turned back to her grandfather. 'I ran into Alesander in San Sebastian,' she said, reeling out the story they'd concocted in the car. Not too many untruths to trip over. 'We got to talking and found out we were neighbours and he offered me a lift home so I didn't have to catch the bus.'

Her grandfather grunted and turned back to look pointedly out of the window towards the land and the vines he'd lost, his message clear, but before he'd turned away she'd seen there was more than resentment in his eyes. There was sadness too, and hurt. Simone turned to their guest and shook her head. He shrugged, as if he'd been expecting such a lack of welcome all along.

'How go the grapes, Felipe?' he asked. 'People are saying it will be the best harvest for years.'

Another grunt from the window.

Alesander gave up. 'I should be going.'

'You won't stay for dinner?' She wasn't sure she wanted him to—the little exchange in the car had left her feeling unsettled—but maybe he'd been expecting to be asked after driving her home. And it would make a change to have younger company for a little while.

He shook his head. 'I won't impose on any more of your time. Felipe, it was good to see you again. It's been too long.'

The old man gave a flick of his gnarled hand without bothering to look around.

'But if there is one favour I might ask you before I go?'

The old man's head turned by only the barest of fractions towards their guest. 'It is Markel de la Silva's sixtieth birthday party on Saturday evening. I was wondering if you might let your granddaughter accompany me.'

The neck that seemed comprised entirely of cords twisted around until his flat glassy eyes met hers. 'Is that what you want?' he asked her pointedly.

'I would love to go,' she said, liking the fact Alesander had asked Felipe for his permission. Their families might have been rivals for years but there was a note of respect in his request that had sounded sincere. Although she wondered what he would do if Felipe said no. 'If it's all right with you, of course.'

Felipe merely grunted. 'You can do what you like, while you are here.'

'In that case, yes,' she said, already panicking about what she would wear. Party dresses hadn't been a high priority on her packing list when she'd come, expecting to stay just a couple of weeks, not that she'd had many to choose from anyway. She'd just have to head into San Sebastian again and find something that would fit into her limited student budget.

Alesander must have been wondering the same thing, a telltale frown bringing his two dark brows closer together as if he could tell from what she was wearing that she would own nothing suitable for a posh Spanish party. 'Did you bring a gown with you?'

A gown? 'No,' she confessed. Although he might just as well have asked if she even possessed a gown. 'But I'm sure I'll find something.'

'I'll take you shopping,' he said. 'Tomorrow. There is work I have to do in the morning first, but shall we say three o'clock?'

'Watch that one,' Felipe said between spooning up his paella. His appetite had been waning lately, and it was the one dish she could guarantee he would do more than pick at. 'Be careful with him.'

'You mean Alesander?' I thought he seemed—' she searched for words that didn't include arrogant and bastard '—very pleasant.'

'You think he is interested in you? Bah! He only came to see how close to death I am.'

'No, Abuelo, why would you say such a thing? Why would he do that?'

'Why else? He is after the vines. He already has three-quarters of them and now he wants the rest, you mark my words.'

She put her fork down, unable to swallow another mouthful, the ball in her stomach like lead and not only weighted with guilt. For, after the agreement she had made with him, Alesander as good as owned the vines. What would her grandfather say if he knew what she had done?

What she had done with good reason, she reminded herself, certain that once the marriage was announced, Felipe would be celebrating to know his precious vines were once again reunited, the fortunes of the Otxoa family restored.

Besides which, did it really matter who owned the vines after Felipe died? It might as well be someone who knew what to do with them.

'I'm sure you're wrong. I know you have had your differences with his father in the past, but

I am sure Alesander is not as ruthless as you make out.'

'He is an Esquivel. Of course he is ruthless!'

'I could have met you in San Sebastian,' she said when Alesander opened the car door for her the next afternoon. 'You didn't have to come all this way.'

'I didn't come for your benefit.' He looked up at the window, where he caught the old man scowling at him before turning his head away. He waved, letting him know he'd seen. 'Felipe needs to get used to seeing us together.'

'Oh,' she said, looking suddenly contrite, 'of course,' before falling quiet as she got into the car, and warning bells went off in his brain. If she was going to start thinking he was being considerate towards her because he was interested in her…

There was no way he wanted her thinking that. He waited until the car was at the end of the driveway so they were well away from the house and Felipe's inquisitive gaze.

'Perhaps I should remind you that we are actors in this masquerade. We are expected to convey an image—first that we are a couple—and second that we are in love.

'But this is a marriage of convenience and it remains a marriage of convenience. A marriage in name only. That's what you wanted and that's what you will get. And if I show you any courtesy, and of course I will because it is all part of the act, it is not because I have suddenly fallen in love with you. It is merely to convince everybody else that I have.'

He looked across at her. 'Do you understand?'

'Yes. Of course I do. My mistake. I'm sorry for ever imagining you were simply being nice.'

He managed a brief smile at her response. On the one hand he found her Australian openness appealing, but at the same time he was concerned at her willingness to embrace something as simple as picking her up from her home as being a sign he cared, and he wondered anew about her long-term plans. She'd said she was doing this all for Felipe, but why should she give up her inheritance for a grumpy old man she barely knew and who he'd never seen happy and would probably never would?

Unless she'd had other plans from the start—other plans that involved making a fake marriage real and trading a modest inheritance for a luxury lifestyle. Was her demand that there be no sex just a way to lull him into a false sense of security?

It had better not be.

'I warn you now, it would be a mistake to ever go thinking I was nice.'

'Don't worry,' she said snippily. 'I won't make the same mistake again.'

CHAPTER FIVE

THE BOUTIQUE WAS just off La Avenida, the main street of San Sebastian, tucked away in a small *calle* closed to motor vehicles, and filled with planter boxes dotted down the *calle* spilling with bushes and greenery while the attractive three- and four-storey buildings that lined the street were home to exclusive boutiques and Michelin-starred restaurants topped by private hotels. The place screamed of money.

Alesander led her towards one of the boutiques now, and she hesitated, thinking of her limited budget. When he'd said he'd take her shopping, she'd imagined he would take her somewhere a little more generic. 'It looks expensive.'

'It is. Only the filthy rich can shop here.'

She stopped completely. There was no way she was setting foot in the place, let alone thinking about buying anything. 'That's not my kind of store.'

'Which is why I brought you. Because I know you could not be trusted to buy the kind of gown you will need to pull this off.'

'But I don't have to step inside to know I can't afford anything in that shop!'

He pulled her aside, leaning down close to her face to keep his words and, no doubt, hopefully hers out of the public realm. 'And we can't afford to get this wrong. If we're going to convince people that you are worthy of being an Esquivel bride, we cannot have you looking like you dressed yourself in some discount department store rags. People would not believe it.' She opened her mouth to protest and he held up one hand, silencing her. '*Especially* not for something as important as Markel's birthday party. Now, we are wasting time.'

'You can't make me go in there—'

'I do not expect you to pay. Of course I will pay. And it will be worth every euro. And, just for the record,' he added for good measure, 'I am not being nice.'

She found the nerve to smile up at him. 'Now that was the one thing I wasn't about to accuse you of.'

She had no time to celebrate her oral victory, for instead she found herself herded, rather than led, into the hushed boutique, where garments hung in spartan clusters around the otherwise minimalist walls. Even so, what was on display was enough that she immediately felt under-dressed, the cut-off capri pants and soft lemon cardigan she'd thought suitable for this shopping expedition now feeling decidedly underdone in this world of hand-printed silks and designer denim.

Not that the two sleek shop attendants seemed to notice or care. They were too busy welcoming Alesander to their store with their wide smiles and gleaming eyes. If he wasn't as good-looking as he was, she'd think they could almost smell his money.

He rattled off something in Spanish too fast for

her to understand and the two women threw a glance her way, sizing her up, chatting excitedly between themselves before one breezed past a rack of gowns and disappeared into a back room while the other introduced them both. Alondra and Evita promised to be of every assistance, she said, nothing would be too much trouble. 'And you are in luck, *señorita*,' the woman called Alondra said excitedly, 'we have some very special gowns delivered just today. They are exclusives. You will not find them anywhere else in all of Spain.'

Her colleague returned a few moments later, her arms laden with four exquisite gowns in rich colours that she hung side by side on a rail to compare. 'What do you think of these?'

They were all different in style, cut and colour, from strapless to asymmetrical to one-shouldered; from lilac to silver to fiery red, but with one thing in common—they were all exquisite.

'Stunning,' she said, overwhelmed by the detail of each of the gowns, whether in the beading or skilful pleating or the soft feminine drape of the skirt, finding it hard to believe that she might soon actually possess anything so beautiful—but, more than that, have an occasion to wear it.

'What about that one?' Alesander said behind her, but when she turned to see which one he meant, he was looking elsewhere, towards an aqua-coloured gown hanging by itself to one side. It was strapless with a pleated bodice, fitted through the body to the hip, where it finished emphatically in a ruffled skirt split high up one thigh. It was dramatic and sexy and seemed to convey the very essence of Spain, understated and yet over the top at the same time. And undeniably the most beautiful dress she'd ever seen.

Ordinarily her eyes would have already bypassed it, knowing there was no point giving it a second glance, knowing there was no way she could afford to even look at it, but these were no ordinary times and besides, she heard him say, 'It would go with your eyes.'

And she shivered and looked back at him uncertainly. When had he noticed the colour of her eyes?

The women descended again into rapid Spanish, to which Alesander simply responded, 'Who?' And when they answered, he smiled and issued a series of instructions to the women and finished with one to her. 'Try it on,' he said.

Heels were produced, and accessories and one woman zipped her into the dress while the other turned her ponytail into a messy knot that looked halfway to evening glam and when she was finally dressed she stared at the result in the mirror. My God, was that really her? Apart from being a little long, the gown fitted her as if it had been made for her, but instead of it emphasising how much weight she had lost in the last few months, like her other clothes did now they were too big, the fact this gown hugged her curves seemed to make the most of them.

'I love it,' she said, wondering at a dress that had the power to transform her from discount department store cheap to designer chic.

'The hem can be altered,' Alondra said. 'That is no problem.'

'And this before make-up and jewellery,' the

other clucked, beaming her delight. 'You must show your boyfriend.'

She almost denied it. Almost said that Alesander wasn't her boyfriend, but stopped herself short. Because he kind of was now, even if it was only make-believe.

He was on the phone when she stepped from the dressing room, his back to her and she said nothing, not wanting to disturb him, but he must have heard something because after a few seconds he stilled and, still talking into his phone, he turned, only for the torrent of words to stop as his dark eyes drank her in. And then he said something short, punched a button to punctuate the call and pocketed the phone.

She smiled nervously, wanting him to like what he saw, if only to show him that she could pull this off. She didn't care what he thought about her, but she did want him to be confident that she could carry off her side of the bargain before they signed the paperwork linking them together. 'What do you think? Will it do for the party?'

It seemed to take an eternity for him to answer, an eternity that had her wondering if he was regretting this deal because she would never be up to the task. '*Sí,*' he said dispassionately at last, 'it will do. And now you will have to excuse me for an hour or so. I have a meeting that will not wait. The *señoritas* have instructions to find you a range of outfits for day and evening and I will leave you in their clearly capable hands.' And with that he was gone.

She clamped down on a bubble of disappointment as she returned to the changing room, the women eagerly rushing around to gather up more garments for her to try on. Alesander approved of the dress. That should be enough. That *was* enough. There was no reason to be disappointed with his reaction.

On the other hand, there was plenty of justification for the resentment that simmered and bubbled away inside her.

Because she'd come here looking for a dress and she'd found one and now he calmly instructed her to find a 'range of outfits'. Clearly he didn't think her existing wardrobe lived up to the necessary Esquivel standards in order to convince the world they were an item. And yes, she understood that the world he inhabited was located somewhere high in the dizzy stratosphere compared to her own, but it still rankled to be so constantly reminded of that fact. It rankled even more to be given instructions without discussion, as if her opinion was not worth either hearing or seeking. After all, they were supposed to be in this together.

'You will be very happy with that gown,' Alondra said.

'Your boyfriend thinks you look very sexy,' said the other.

He still wasn't her boyfriend and she very much doubted he thought about how she looked other than to gauge whether she would pass muster and be accepted in his company. 'Well, he sure didn't say much.'

'Didn't you see his eyes?' The women looked at each other with a smile. 'His eyes, they said plenty. He thought you were hot.'

Shop girl talk, she figured as she slipped out of the dress, the same the world over and designed to make you feel good about whatever you were trying on. If they saw anything in his eyes, it was most likely the greedy prospect of getting his hands on the rest of Felipe's vines.

Besides, he didn't think her hot. She wasn't his type and that was fine. That was good. It made it so much easier to deal with him, knowing he wasn't in the least bit interested in her.

She only wished she could be as impartial to him. Maybe then she wouldn't spend so much time thinking how good he'd looked dressed only in a towel. And God, how he had. And then there was his evocative scent and the curl of his long tapered fingers around the steering wheel and the way her skin had sizzled when they touched…

No, thank God he wasn't interested in her because it made the whole no-sex deal workable. Knowing the terms of their contract would stipulate that condition was comforting. But knowing she could rely on him not to try anything was the clincher.

At least one of them would be thinking straight.

His meeting had been interminable as plans were made for the upcoming harvest, and he wondered at the sense of leaving her for so long with a blank credit card. But she wasn't still shopping. Instead, he found the three women sitting at a table outside the nearby restaurant, eating pintxos and sipping on Mojitos. 'I do hope,' he said, joining them and only half joking, 'this doesn't mean Simone has bought everything in the shop.'

She coloured and gave a guilty smile, as if she'd been caught in the act, and he smiled too, not just because he couldn't remember the last time he'd seen a woman blush, but because somehow she looked different. She'd changed her top—out of whatever nondescript rag she'd been wearing before, for a flirty silk blouse patterned in orange and teal that he liked—but he was sure there was something else.

'It's our fault,' one of the shop assistants said. 'We have kept Simone so busy, we felt she deserved a treat.'

'So busy,' the other said, 'but so efficient that we even managed to get her into the salon across the street. Do you like Simone's new look?'

So that was what was different about her? Now he could see not only that her hair had been professionally styled, but that highlights had been added, whisper-thin streaks of chilli and cinnamon that gleamed in the light and blended in with the natural honey-gold of her hair. Somehow it seemed to give her hair depth. He nodded. 'I approve.'

'I won't hold you up,' she said, her cheeks flaring now under his scrutiny as she awkwardly stood, reaching for her shopping.

'Is that all there is?' he asked, surveying the small collection of carrier bags nearby.

'The gown needs to be taken up,' said one of the women, 'It will be delivered tomorrow.'

'But that's the rest of it?'

One of the women laughed. 'Your girlfriend

is a very reluctant shopper, *señor.* We tried to convince her but she would not buy a fraction of what we picked out for her.' She nodded. 'You are a very lucky man.'

The women excused themselves to return to their shop while she gathered up her bags.

He leaned past her to collect up the last of them and he breathed in her scent, like warm peaches on a sunny day. Liking her perfume, even though it was probably just the shampoo the salon had used. Still, he liked the changes he was noticing about her. She was still not his type, but it would make it so much easier to pretend. 'They think we are a couple.'

'I know. I couldn't see the point of correcting them.'

'No, it is good,' he said, leading her back to where he'd parked the car. 'That is what everyone is meant to think. If they assume simply because we are seen shopping together that we are a couple, imagine what people will believe when they see us kiss.'

See us kiss? 'You *were* actually fitting me out

with a wardrobe,' she said, trying to find a shred of logic in a mind that wanted to hone in and focus on the prospect of him kissing her instead. When? How? *How soon?* 'We weren't "simply shopping" at all.'

He shrugged. 'Still, I think we will have no trouble convincing people.'

They were almost at Getaria when she remembered to ask, 'What was that about in the shop before, when you first asked about the dress?'

He looked across at her. 'When?'

'You said something like "What about that one?" after they brought the first batch of gowns over and that one was set apart. But you were all speaking so fast, I couldn't understand.'

He shook his head. 'I don't understand what you're asking. We have the dress, don't we?'

'I mean, was there a reason they didn't include it in the first place? Did they think it wouldn't suit me?'

'Ah,' he said. 'Apparently another of their clients had expressed interest in seeing it, that was all.'

'Oh, you mean they had it reserved for someone?'

He shrugged. 'It makes no difference now.'

'But won't that person be disappointed that it's sold?'

He smiled. 'Probably.'

She settled back into her seat, tangling fingers in her lap, newly manicured fingernails painted bright red if he wasn't mistaken. He had to hand it to her, she had been busy this afternoon.

'I should thank you, of course,' she said, 'for the clothes and everything.'

'I'm not sure you got anywhere near enough.'

'You must be kidding,' she said with a shake of her head, 'there's heaps, really there is. I just hate to think how much it cost. But in case you're wondering, I paid for the salon. I don't want you thinking I'd take advantage…'

Was she serious? Or was this just another tactic to lull him into taking her and her story at face value and believing she wanted nothing more than to make an old man die happy? Because none of the women he knew were anywhere near as naive or horrified at the prospect of spending someone else's money on themselves.

But then none of the women he knew would go to such extraordinary lengths that she was going either. Why was she going to such trouble for her grandfather? He didn't like that he didn't know, but if he ended up with the vines and she ended up not pregnant and with no claim on the estate, he didn't really care.

What he did like was the way she blushed. Whether it was because of her fair colouring, or because she was harbouring some guilty secret, that was one thing he wasn't used to. He glanced sideways at her. And he liked whatever the salon had done to her hair and how the sunlight through his roof turned her highlights to glistening threads of copper and gold. Not that he was about to admit that to her.

In fact, given his misgivings about her motives, he was better off not giving her too much encouragement at all.

He changed down gears as he headed into a

tight bend, changing down gears on his thoughts at the same time.

'You might want to save your money,' he said, probably sounding more gruff than he intended, 'for when you get home. You might need it.'

Cold.

He might just as well have tossed a bucket of icy water over her. And why?

Moreover, why did she even care?

Alesander was nothing to her but a solution to a problem.

She was nothing to him but a means to an end.

It was a mutual arrangement.

So why did he feel it so important to remind her that this arrangement was not permanent?

Didn't he think that was how she wanted it?

She turned to him, or rather to his profile, strong and noble and too utterly perfect to be real, as he negotiated the winding track up the hill towards her grandfather's vineyard. 'What are you so afraid of?'

'What do you mean?'

'Only that every chance you get, you feel the

need to remind me that this arrangement is temporary. "You might want to save your money for when you get home," you said. Well, I do know this is temporary because I was the one who insisted it would be from the start.'

'I don't know what you're talking about.'

'Just that you seem to be operating under the misapprehension that I either want or expect this arrangement to become permanent.'

He scoffed her protests away. 'I have only your word that you don't want it to be.'

'I am expecting to sign a contract saying exactly that! A contract which includes the condition *I* specifically demanded when I brokered this agreement—a condition that precludes sex between us. So when will you believe me? Because as clearly wonderful a catch as you so evidently are, I would rather not have to marry you. I don't want to be your wife, other than to convince Felipe that his vines are as good as reunited. And when Felipe is no longer with us, I expect the quickest divorce from marriage with you that it is possible to get. I expect the contract terms to reflect that fact.'

He changed down gears as he rounded the bend before climbing the hill up towards Felipe's estate. 'I will ensure it will be provided as quick as is humanly or inhumanly possible. I will not make you wait to be free.'

'Excellent. So we understand each other then.'

'Oh yes,' he said through gritted teeth, 'we understand each other perfectly.'

The banging started the next morning while she was cooking breakfast. 'What is that?' a grumpy Felipe demanded, peering out of the window, searching for the cause.

'I don't know,' she answered as she put a plate of eggs on the table for him. 'I'll go and find out.'

The morning air was crisp and clean. It would be warm later, but for now the cool air prickled the skin of her bare arms and her nipples turned to tight buds. She should have grabbed her jacket before she'd set off, she thought, hugging her arms over her chest as she followed the sound down the driveway.

Around a bend she found a four-wheel drive parked and someone working under the vines where part of the trellis had collapsed under the weight of the vines. And she remembered that Alesander had said something about getting that fixed. She hadn't paid any heed to his words at the time but he must have meant it and sent someone after all, no doubt to ensure there was no more damage done before he took over the vineyard completely.

But even if he was doing it for his own reasons, she could still be hospitable.

'*Buenos dias,*' she called out over the hammering. 'Is there anything you need that I can get you?'

'Coffee would be good,' a familiar deep voice said, as Alesander pushed aside the tangle of vines with one arm to peer out at her.

'You? What are you doing here?'

'I told you I'd get this fixed.'

'But I thought you'd send someone. I didn't expect you.'

'Well, you got me.'

His eyes raked over her and her bullet-hard nipples suddenly had nothing to do with the cold because she was suddenly feeling hot.

'I'll get you that coffee,' she said, discomfited, her cheeks flaring with heat.

He smiled as she turned away. 'You do that.'

'Who is it?' asked Felipe as she returned to the cottage. 'Who's making all that noise?'

She poured coffee into a mug. 'It's Alesander. He's fixing some of the broken trellising.'

'Why? What is he doing meddling with my vines?' He swayed backwards and forwards in his chair, gaining momentum and looking as if he was intending to get up and go and take issue with him. 'They're not his to meddle with!'

'Abuelo,' she said with her hands to his shoulders, squeezing gently, feeling a pang of guilt in her chest, knowing that soon they would be his to do anything he liked with them, 'he's being neighbourly, that's all.'

'Neighbourly? Pah!' But he settled back in his chair, already wheezing under the strain of his efforts.

'Yes, neighbourly. It's about time this feud between the Esquivels and the Oxtoas was put to bed once and for all, don't you think?'

He muttered something in Basque under his breath. Normally she'd ask him what he meant, but not this time. This time she had a fairly good idea what he meant without the translation. 'I'm taking Alesander some coffee. I'll be back soon.'

'It's the vines,' he called out in his thin voice as she left. 'He doesn't want you.'

She didn't answer. Felipe might be right, but she didn't have to tell him that. Not when she needed him soon to believe the exact opposite.

Alesander was busy under the vines when she returned, intent on the task of replacing a broken upright, and she leant against his car and watched him work. She hadn't pegged him as someone good at manual work, but he seemed to know what he was doing, every action purposeful and certain.

She watched him manhandle the new post into position, liking the way his body worked and the muscles bunched in his arms.

She watched him twisting broken wire together, increasing the tension on the wire supporting the heavy vines.

He was good with his hands.

And then she deliberately looked away while he finished the job, turning her gaze towards the view out to sea because she didn't want to think of the man having clever hands, not when that was something she didn't need to know.

It was better not to know.

It would be better if she didn't think about it.

What was it about this man who turned her thoughts carnal when her intentions were anything but? Thank God he'd agreed that there would be no sex between them. Never again would she have sex with a man who didn't love her one hundred per cent. Never again would she experience that sickening fear that she might be carrying the child of a man she didn't love with all her heart.

She wouldn't let it happen.

'Is that for me?' he asked, startling her, so lost in her thoughts she hadn't heard him approach. She turned to see the job done, the once fallen vines now lifted high off the ground again.

'Oh, yes,' she said, handing him the mug, pulling her hand away quickly when their fingers brushed. He sipped the coffee, thoughtfully watching her, and nodded.

'*Bueno*. How's Felipe this morning?'

'Mistrustful. He wonders what you're about.'

Alesander smiled. 'He'll come around,' and put the coffee to his lips again—good lips, wide and not at all thin—and she suddenly felt awkward, standing here, watching a man drink a cup of coffee. She wondered if she should go. She'd delivered the promised coffee after all. Then again, she'd only have to come back for the cup…

'Why are the vines grown so high?' she asked, finally falling on something to say. 'It must make looking after them more difficult.'

He shrugged. 'It's the way here. The weather

from the sea can be harsh. This way the vines form a canopy that protects the fruit beneath, making it more suitable for the grapes to flourish. And of course—' he smiled '—up high they get a much better view of the sea.'

And she blinked as she remembered a phrase from her childhood, a sliver of a memory she'd forgotten until now, some words an old man had told her as she'd trailed behind him around the vineyard asking endless questions while he'd snipped and trimmed the vines, answering her in faltering Spanglish. He'd told her his grapes were magic grapes and she'd asked him what made them magic and he'd told her what made them magic.

'The sparkle of the sea.'

His eyes narrowed as he regarded her. '*Sí*. The grapes with the view make the best wine. They say that is why our *txakoli* wine sparkles when it is poured.'

'Is it true?'

'Of course it is true. And also it is to do with the fermentation process as well. But why wouldn't grapes be happy with a view such as this?'

They stood together for a moment, looking out over the vista, as the vine-covered hillside fell away to the low rolling countryside to the coast. And the sea did indeed sparkle under the morning sun, just as her skin tingled where it was touched by the heat of him.

'But I am boring you,' he said. 'When you care nothing for the vines. Thank you for the coffee. I should get back to work here.'

She took the cup, still warm, cradling it in her hands. She didn't care for the vines. And yet there was something about them that tugged at her. Maybe it was just the remnants of a short time in her childhood when the vineyard had been her playground. 'Surely you have more important things to do? I thought you had a business to run.'

'I grew up doing this work. I like it and these days I so rarely get a chance to do it. But it is good to be closer to the grapes.'

'How are they—can you tell?' And she surprised herself by caring to know the answer, even as she knew she was putting off returning to the house. 'Do you think there will be any point harvesting them?'

He nodded and looked back at the vines above his shoulder, where bunches of small grapes hung down from the vines. She tried to look at the grapes and not the Vee of skin at his neck where his white shirt lay open. She couldn't help but notice the man made an innocent white shirt look positively sinful, the way it pulled over his shoulders and turned olive skin darker. 'It would be a crime not to pick them. The vines should have been pruned in the winter, of course, which is why they are such a mess now, but they are good vines—old but strong—they have still produced good fruit. Has Felipe had the grapes tested at all?'

She looked blankly back at him.

'No,' he said, 'I assumed not. But soon they should be tested for their sugar and acidity levels. That will tell when they are right for harvest.

But it is only a matter of weeks. Two, maybe three at the most.'

Her teeth found her lip. She shook her head. 'Could I manage it, do you think? I've never done anything like this before.'

'You can help, but the job will be bigger than just you.'

She smiled stiffly. 'Will you talk to Felipe about it, then? You know so much more than me about what is needed to be done.'

'You think he will listen to me?'

'At least you speak the same language. With me, our conversations are limited to the basics. I want him to see that all is not lost, that life goes on, that the vines go on.'

'Then I will talk with him. I will come up to the house before I go.'

'Thank you.'

She turned to leave but he caught her hand. 'I could ask you the same question.' And when he caught her frown, 'Why are you doing this?'

'You know already. So he has a chance to smile before he dies.'

'*Sí.*' He nodded. 'But why? Why do you care so about a grumpy old man who lives halfway around the world and who you barely know? Why have you given up an inheritance for him?'

She smiled at the 'grumpy old man' reference. There was no point in objecting to that. 'He's all I have left in the world.'

'Is that enough to do what you are doing? I ask myself if it is enough and still it makes no sense. Why do you care so much?'

Why did she care? She turned her face up to the wide blue sky. And suddenly she was back, that seven-year-old child with long tangled hair and an even more tangled family and a promise she'd made when her screaming mother had wrenched her in tears from her grandmother's arms, their one brief attempt at bridge-building over, with a vow never to see them again.

Simone had witnessed the pain in her grandmother's eyes, had witnessed the anguish in her grandfather's and understood nothing of what was going on, except the raw agony that these new people in her life—people that she had grown to love and know that they were important to her—were feeling.

Anguish that had transferred to her.

'My parents brought me to Spain when I was seven,' she said. 'Felipe paid the fares. He was trying to reach out to my mother but, of course, I know he wanted to meet me too, as his only grandchild. The visit started well. I remember a week or two of relative peace—or maybe they were just trying to hide the worst from me as a child—but then it ended badly. It was always bound to end badly.'

Horribly.

She could still hear her father's shouting and accusations. She could still hear her mother's shrill cries that she had never been welcome in her own home.

And most of all she could remember the look of desolation on Felipe's and Maria's faces as she'd been ripped from their arms, as if they knew this was the last time they would ever lay eyes on any of them ever again.

She hadn't understood what was going on, but

she'd been torn. She'd loved them all and she couldn't understand why they couldn't love each other. And she couldn't understand the hurt. She would make up for it one day, she'd promised then and there. She would come back and make up for their pain.

'I said I'd come back,' she said. 'In the midst of all the shrieking, I promised them I'd return.'

'You did,' Alesander said. 'You're here now.'

She dipped her shaking head. No. She'd meant to come back years before now. She'd meant to return when she was old enough to make the travel plans herself. But life and university and lack of funds had meant that promises of years gone by were overtaken by the needs of the present. She would still go back to Getaria, she'd repeatedly told herself—one day.

Except that she hadn't. She'd let life get in the way of good intentions. And now Maria had died without ever seeing her again, and Felipe was dying too.

And good intentions, she realised, were not

enough. Not when guilt that she had done noth-ing weighed so heavily upon her.

'I'll see you back at the house,' she said.

He watched her go, lonely and sad, and just for a moment he was almost tempted to go to her. But why? What would he say? They were nothing to each other, even if he understood why she was doing what she was doing a little more.

But her demons were her own.

It was not his job to fix them.

CHAPTER SIX

'HE'S HERE AGAIN,' Felipe growled as Alesander arrived for the sixth time in as many days, but this time his voice contained less censure, more tolerance. Alesander had called by the vineyard every day. On one day he'd brought the contracts for her to sign and she'd read them in the privacy of his car parked out of sight, carefully checking to ensure the agreement included all the terms she'd asked for—the no sex clause, the termination, the consideration. Then, and only then, she'd put her signature to the contract.

But every day he'd stopped by the house to talk to Felipe and always finding something to repair while he was there, and for all his gruffness, the old man was enjoying talking to another man, she could tell.

'Of course, he's here, Abuelo,' she said, emerging from her room. 'He's come to take me to the party. How do I look?'

Felipe craned his head around and blinked, his jaw sagging open. 'What have you done with Simone?'

'It is me,' she protested before she caught the glint in her grandfather's eyes and realised he was joking, the first time she'd heard him joke since she'd arrived. 'Oh, Abuelo,' she said, laughing, giving his shoulders a squeeze, trying to stop a tear squeezing from her eyes and ruin her eye make-up, 'stop teasing.'

'Who's teasing?' Alesander said from the open front door.

'Felipe, the old rogue,' she said without looking up. 'He's wondering what I've done with Simone.' And then she lifted her head and saw him, in a dark-as-night evening suit and snow-white shirt, his dark hair rippling back from his sculpted face. Her mouth went dry. He looked— *amazing*.

'You'd better go tell her to hurry up,' Alesander said, 'I don't want to be late for Markel's party.'

Felipe snorted beside her while Alesander's mouth turned upwards into a smile.

She smiled back, a smile of thanks. 'I'll just go and get her in that case,' and went to fetch her wrap.

'Don't keep her out too late,' she heard Felipe tell him. 'She's a good girl.'

'Don't give away all my secrets, Abuelo,' she gently chided, dipping her head to kiss his grizzled cheeks. 'And you behave yourself while I'm out.'

Markel's home looked more like a palace than any house she had ever had reason to visit, complete with porticoes and balconies and tall arched windows and doors, and all lit up so the pale walls turned to gold against the evening sky, every open window glowing a warm welcome. Strategically placed palm trees softened the bold lines of the exterior while a fountain tinkled musically in the centre of the driveway turnaround.

'Help,' she said softly to herself as he pulled the

car up next to waiting doormen who smoothly
pulled open their doors. She'd known she was
out of her depth from the first time she'd looked
up at Alesander's apartment, but once again she
was reminded just how far. This was a world
where houses were palatial and came complete
with tinkling fountains and where uniformed
men waited on you hand and foot. This was so
not her world.

She took a deep breath, careful not to trip on
her gown, as she stepped from the car. There
was music coming from inside, and the hum
of conversation punctuated with the occasional
peal of laughter, the note of which seemed to
match the tinkling fountain. 'Nervous?' he said
as he joined her, while his car was whisked away
behind them for parking by the valet.

She nodded and smiled tightly, her fingers biting down on her evening purse. This was it. The
night she not only met his family and friends,
but paved the way for him presenting her soon
as his fiancée.

Of course she was nervous.

'Relax,' he told her, his eyes massaging her fears away. 'Tonight you look like you were born to this. You look every inch an Esquivel bride. You look beautiful.'

She blinked up at him. Did he really mean it or was it just one more of his build-her-up pep talks to make her believe they could do this—before he pulled the rug out from under her feet again, just in case she actually got to thinking this could become permanent?

He'd barely spoken in the car after she'd thanked him for playing along with Felipe's joke and she'd guessed it was because he didn't have an audience he needed to impress any more.

'It's true,' he said, as if he was attuned to her unsaid thoughts and fears, his face perilously close to hers as he squeezed her hand so hard that she almost felt as if she wanted to believe him. But this was Alesander, she reminded herself. Alesander wasn't in the business of being nice. He bestowed upon her courtesies to convince everyone else that they were a couple, and he needed her to believe enough to carry it off.

Nothing more.

And that was *exactly* the way she wanted it. Business, she reminded herself, taking a deep breath. This is business. She could do this if she remembered it was business. 'Okay,' she said with a determination she wished would stop wavering, 'I'm ready. Let's get this show on the road.'

But if arriving at Markel's home had been daunting, inside was terrifying. So many people, so many women, all of whom seemed to know Alesander. All of whom were apparently keen to discover who she was.

Right now she might just as well have been a butterfly stuck with a pin inside a display case.

'Alesander, you came.' A woman's voice broke through the laughter. 'I knew you would.'

He leaned down and they kissed, cheek to cheek. 'Of course, Madre, I wouldn't have missed it for the world.'

The woman's gaze didn't linger on her son, moving at laser speed over his guest, appraisal, judgement and summary execution in one rapier-sharp movement. 'Oh, I see you found another cleaner.'

Cleaner? She looked up at him, waiting for an explanation, but Alesander only laughed.

'Allow me to introduce you to Simone Hamilton, granddaughter of Felipe. Simone, my mother, Isobel Esquivel.'

Simone's greeting was cut off, her proffered hand left hanging.

'Felipe?'

'Felipe Otxoa—our neighbour in Getaria. Remember?'

'Oh, *that* Felipe. I didn't realise he had a granddaughter.'

'I'm from Australia,' Simone offered in her rusty Spanish. 'I haven't been here long.'

The older woman smiled for the first time. 'Oh,' she said, giving Simone's hand the briefest of acknowledgements with hers, 'I hope you enjoy your holiday,' and took Alesander's arm, effectively excluding her from the conversation as she turned away to look for someone in the crowd. 'By the way, darling, have you seen Ezmerelda yet? She looks fabulous tonight.'

Simone hooked a glass of champagne from a passing tray and almost had it to her mouth before Alesander claimed her arm and drew her back into the group. Wine sloshed over the rim of her glass at the sudden change of direction. His mother noticed, sending her a look of *oh-you-so-don't-belong-here*, and she thought how terrified she'd be if Isobel was to be her real mother-in-law. Fortunately she didn't have to be terrified.

'Alesander's always grabbing me at inopportune times,' she shared with a conspiratorial smile. 'It's quite embarrassing.'

As if to agree, he smiled and pulled her in close to his body. She didn't mind the display of affection. Not really. Other than what it did to her internal thermostat. But she could imagine worse places to be than against the hard wall of his body. And it was for a good cause. 'Simone is actually staying a while,' he said. 'As long as Felipe needs help.'

His mother looked anywhere but at the places they made contact. 'What's wrong with Felipe?'

'He's ill, I'm afraid. He's not doing so well lately.' For a moment she almost thought she saw something like sympathy reflected in the older woman's eyes but just as swiftly it was gone as she caught sight of someone in the crowd. 'Oh, there she is. Alesander, I'll be right back.'

'So who's Ezmerelda?' she asked, easing herself away from the disturbing proximity of his body heat when his mother was out of earshot. 'Should I be afraid?'

'Markel's daughter, to answer your first question, and probably a resounding yes to the second.'

'And why, exactly, should I be afraid of her?'

He leaned close to her ear and whispered, 'Because you're wearing her dress.'

Shock forced her jaw to fall open. She stared at him, disbelieving. 'What? So you knew all the time who wanted this dress? What kind of person would do that?'

'A person who thought the dress would be

wasted on her and look better on you. And it would have been and it does. Much better.'

She barely had time to digest that justification—for she could hardly call it a compliment, surely—when his mother was back with two people in tow. 'Here they are,' she said. 'I told you Ezmerelda looked fabulous.'

Simone caught her breath. Not just fabulous, but stunning as she smiled a greeting to another couple as she passed, her bearing regal if not haughty, looking every inch a Spanish society princess with her black hair pulled back and woven into an intricate up-do, and wide dark eyes and flawless skin. Simone felt pale and uninteresting in comparison.

Markel reached them first, bowing a ruddy-cheeked face lower to catch her name, his smile wide as she wished him a happy birthday before he drifted off into the crowd for more congratulations. She liked the man on sight.

And then Ezmerelda turned her head and her smile widened as her gaze fell on Alesander, a smile that slid away when her eyes found her standing alongside, especially when she saw what she was wearing. Simone saw confusion in her beautiful eyes, and anger and something else that looked like hurt, and she wished the floor would open up and swallow her whole.

'Alesander,' she said, turning away once she'd recovered, 'how lovely of you to come.'

They kissed cheeks. 'You're looking beautiful, as usual, Ezmerelda. I'd like you to meet Simone Hamilton.'

'How lovely you brought a friend,' she said with barely a glance in her direction, 'but then when do you not have a friend? You're simply too popular, Alesander.'

She wanted to run. It was like being in a lion's den with a lioness whose cub she was trying to steal. A hungry lioness. But Alesander wouldn't let her run. He had her pinned in tight next to his body and he wasn't letting her go.

It was a relief when a band started playing. 'Ah,' Ezmerelda said, 'the tango display is about to begin, a special treat for my father. I must find him.'

Simone almost sagged with relief, thankful now that he had such a tight hold on her.

'Come,' he said, ushering her to a balcony overlooking the floor below, where two dancers posed dramatically, metres apart, on the marble floor. The woman was stunning, her gown like a sheath that flared into a sequin-studded skirt slit to the hip. The man looked equally potent.

And they watched as the music became more dramatic and the dancers circled each other almost warily before starting their attack. And it almost seemed like an attack to Simone—a chase, a seduction, rejection and sex. The dance was unmistakably about sex.

She felt it through each dramatic gesture, each silken caress, all of them purposeful and part of the game. They were exhilarating. But the last was the best, the music evocative and sexy and the dancers, now gleaming in the light with sweat, turned the music physical with their bodies. 'What is this music?' she whispered, moved by its powerful emotion.

'It's called *Sentimientos*,' he whispered back,

close to her ear, his warm breath fanning her ear and throat while his thumb traced lazy circles on the back of her hand. 'It means feelings.'

It didn't surprise her. It was the most beautiful music she had ever heard.

Just as the dancers' physical expression of the music was the sexiest thing she had ever seen. She felt breathless with the spectacle, and never before had she been so acutely aware of the man standing beside her, of his steady breathing, of all the places where their bodies touched.

She liked how it felt.

She hated that she liked it.

And when the dancing was over and Alesander released her to applaud, she took the opportunity to flee to the powder room, closing the door behind her and hushing out the sounds of the party. She leaned both hands on the counter and breathed deep. She would have to go back out soon and smile and try to look relaxed, as if she was enjoying herself, but for now, for just a few short moments, she didn't have to pretend.

She heard the door open and close behind her

but didn't bother looking up. It wasn't as if she knew anyone. 'I like your gown.'

Except maybe her.

She opened her eyes. Ezmerelda was standing by the door, watching her. Would it be paranoid of her to think the woman had followed her in here? She tossed up whether or not to apologise, to say she hadn't known it was her dress when they'd bought it, but that would mean she knew and maybe it was more politic to pretend to know nothing. 'Thank you. As it happens, I like yours.'

She shrugged the compliment aside. 'In fact I almost bought one similar to yours recently. Remarkably similar, in fact. Until I decided it was too trashy for such a significant event such as this. It suits you, though.'

Ouch. Mind you, she could hardly blame Ezmerelda being irate after the stunt Alesander had pulled. Not that it meant she'd take this woman's ire lying down.

'What a coincidence,' she replied evenly. 'I do

believe I saw one like yours too. But I decided this one was so much sexier.'

Ezmerelda's eyes glittered as she swept a path to the counter, digging a lipstick from her purse, touching it to her blood-red lips. 'I expect Alesander bought it for you?'

Simone smiled at the other woman. Did anyone here not believe it? She shrugged. 'So what if he did?'

'You're sleeping with him then.' She nodded. 'I thought as much.'

Simone didn't bother denying it as Ezmerelda calmly went back to checking her make-up. She'd clearly made up her mind and, besides, wasn't that what they wanted people to think? And then, just as abruptly, the woman stopped preening and stared at her in the mirror.

'I like you, Simone. You don't pretend to be anything that you're not and I really do understand. You sleep with him—he buys you a dress and takes you to a big party. It's a simple arrangement. I can see the appeal.' She shrugged.

'And because you have been honest with me, I, in turn, will be honest with you.'

'I appreciate it.' Simone waited as the other woman reshaped two perfectly arched eyebrows with her finger.

'Alesander likes his women. Everybody knows that. But everybody here also knows that family comes first, whatever distractions he finds along the way.' She tilted her head and smiled sympathetically. 'And believe me, there have been plenty of distractions along the way. But our two families have always had an understanding and perhaps you should also understand. Alesander and I are to be married.'

Really? Funny how Alesander hadn't mentioned that little fact along the way. 'Do you love him?' she ventured uneasily. She suspected not— Ezmerelda didn't look as if she was pining for a man who didn't seem to know she was alive, but she'd already inadvertently stolen a gown out from under her. She didn't want someone's broken heart on her conscience as well. That hadn't been part of her plans.

For a moment the other woman looked perplexed. 'I like him, yes, and it is a good match,' she said before nodding, as if agreeing with her own words. 'Together our families will create a new dynasty. He will love me, of course.'

Simone found a smile for Ezmerelda and this time it was genuine. What kind of life must she have, waiting for a man who showed no inclination to marry her—indeed, who flaunted his women in front of her? 'Then I do understand. Thank you so much for taking the time to share that with me.'

The Spanish woman sighed and swivelled in front of the mirror, checking the view from every angle, before snapping her purse closed, her smile back on and in full force. 'I'm so pleased we had this little chat. I should get back to the party now.'

'You should,' Simone agreed as the other woman headed for the door. 'Oh, and Ezmerelda?'

'*Sí?*'

'You look stunning in that gown. You are far

and away the most beautiful woman here to-night.'

And the other woman smiled. '*Sí*,' she said, and slipped out of the room, leaving Simone staring blankly at the door, trying to get her head together. Alesander had asked if she had a boyfriend, but she hadn't thought to ask him if there was someone in his life who would be upset by his marriage. She'd assumed he would never have said yes if there was.

But now there was Ezmerelda, who clearly thought she was first in line to marry him. And she might not love him, she might be all kinds of crazy to wait for a man who clearly had no intention of marrying her, but when their engagement was announced, she was going to be devastated.

How could she do this?

'I thought I'd lost you,' Alesander said when finally she emerged from the powder room, handing her a fresh glass of wine before walking her slowly towards French windows that led to a terrace overlooking the garden.

'I would have been back much sooner, but your girlfriend and apparently my new best friend wanted to have a little heart-to-heart with me.'

'My girlfriend?'

She rolled her eyes. Were there so many of them that he lost track? 'Ezmerelda, of course.'

'About the dress?'

She sipped her wine as she stepped out into the balmy night air and a courtyard strung with fairy lights. 'Words were spoken about the dress, it's true, although strangely enough the main topic of the conversation was you.'

'Should I be worried?'

The lights reflected in his eyes, turning them playful. She wanted to smack him.

'I was warned off you because apparently your families have an "understanding" and you're practically betrothed. Imagine my surprise.'

He took her hand in his and lifted it to his mouth, his hot lips like a brand upon her skin. 'Imagine Ezmerelda's surprise when she learns that we are to be married.'

She pulled her hand away, wishing he wouldn't

do that thing with her hand and his mouth. Wishing even more that she didn't shiver every time he did.

'You're not planning on telling her our arrangement is only temporary, then?'

'Why would I do that?'

'Why wouldn't you, if you cared anything for this woman who claims to be the next best thing to your fiancèe? Unless, of course, you don't care anything for her. Then again, given you're the man who bought the dress she had reserved for another woman to wear to the same party and then stood back to watch the fireworks, I'd conclude you don't care much for her at all. I'd even be willing to conclude you don't even like her.'

He looked around, checking to make sure they were not overheard, before dipping his head and continuing in a low voice that rumbled over her skin. 'Let's just say Ezmerelda is not my idea of a happily ever after, whatever our respective mothers may have concocted during their regular coffee mornings.'

She shrugged the stroke of voice on skin away.

'So you really played me for a fool. You didn't really need the vines to seal this deal at all, did you?'

'Excuse me?'

'That whole "What's in it for me?" argument of yours was a crock all along. My proposal was just what you needed to get Ezmerelda off your back.'

'I am quite capable of dealing with Ezmerelda with or without your intervention.'

'But marrying me does provide you with a handy out. She can't marry you if you've already got a wife. I bet you're hoping she's got her talons in someone else before our marriage is over.'

'I admit there may have been an element of that in my deliberations.'

'So I didn't have to sign over the vines at all. There was already plenty in it for you.'

'But you did sign them over.'

'But if I'd known about Ezmerelda—'

'That's just it,' he said, downing the rest of his glass and placing it on the tray of a passing waiter. 'You didn't.'

She turned away, feeling as if she'd been duped. Worse, she felt used. She'd thought they'd negotiated a deal when he'd held all the cards to begin with. Felipe had told her to watch him and he was right. Alesander was as ruthless as they came.

And it didn't matter to know that her future waited for her half a world away. A vineyard halfway up a mountain in northern Spain was no good to her as it was, but she could have sold it. Alesander would have bought it, even if it was overgrown and neglected. She could have got something for it. Instead she'd practically given it to him and now she'd be going home as penniless as when she'd arrived.

'Cheer up,' he said. 'You don't look like you're having fun.'

'Oh, I am,' she lied. 'I'm having immense fun debating when to confide to my new best friend that all is not lost, that maybe things aren't as dire as they seem and that she may well still get her man, slightly used but none the worse for wear. But do I tell her before the wedding, or after?'

He bristled. She saw it in the flex of his shoulders and the set of a jaw that had gone from smug to stiff in a heartbeat. 'You wouldn't dare risk the news getting out and getting back to Felipe.'

'You're right, I wouldn't. But it was so worth the look on your face to say it.'

'You have a strange sense of humour, Miss Hamilton.'

'Miss Hamilton? We are formal, aren't we? I suspect I must have made you angry for some reason.'

'On the contrary, but you do have a habit of taking me by surprise at times.'

'Do I? That's actually a good thing, isn't it? It would be awful being stuck together for even ten minutes if we bored each other senseless.'

Oh, there was no chance of that, he thought.

'Anyway,' she continued, 'I won't have to tell Ezmerelda anything, because you're going to tell her that you're getting married and to someone else first.'

'What?'

'Before you make any public announcement of our impending marriage, you will take Ezmerelda aside and let her know that we are getting married. And I don't care what you think of her or what kind of person she might be, she deserves to hear it from you first. She deserves that much consideration at least.'

Now he was angry. He looked down at her coldly. He wasn't used to being told what to do, let alone by a pint-sized woman who without her spiky heels barely came up to his shoulder. But, worst of all, he supposed she might actually be right. The last thing they needed when he made the announcement was a scene.

Though he'd wager that wasn't what was motivating Simone. If he didn't know better, he'd actually think she felt sorry for Ezmerelda, which made no sense at all, given the way she hadn't hesitated to warn her off.

And that was something new. As far as he

knew, she'd never done that before. Or maybe nobody else had ever been game enough to tell him. This woman was, not to mention game enough to tell him to put her out of her misery as part of the deal. His doorstep bride really was turning out to be a surprise package indeed.

He looked around at the thinning crowd. He'd thought about making the announcement tonight when there were still enough people to witness the news to guarantee its rapid spread, but Simone did have a point. He didn't want to ruin Markel's party by creating a scene.

'Will you be all right if I leave you for a few minutes?'

She raised one eyebrow in question—a question he chose to ignore. 'I'll be fine. And look, here comes Markel.' The older man joined them, his ruddy cheeks even redder, his greying hair spiking up above one ear. 'Markel,' she said, 'I don't suppose you could look after me while Alesander runs off to take care of some business?'

'Gladly,' he said, looping her arm through his.

'Nothing would give me greater pleasure. You can tell me all about Australia. Tell me, is it true they sell wine in cardboard boxes there?'

'It is true, though it created all sorts of problems in the industry.'

'Oh,' he said, all ears. 'Why is that?'

'Nobody could work out how to make square grapes.'

It was the lamest attempt at a joke she'd ever made, but Markel roared with laughter, his good birthday humour clearly alcohol assisted.

Remarkable, Alesander thought as he drifted out of earshot, searching the crowd for a familiar face—now she told jokes? What other hidden talents did the woman possess?

There were some that weren't so much hidden as suggested. Just thinking of her in that dress, there were some he wouldn't mind having revealed. From the moment he'd arrived to pick her up and seen her wearing it again, the split from toe to thigh over one leg and the bodice wrapped low over her breasts, he'd wanted to do nothing more than to peel it off. He'd stewed the whole way here, wondering how he was going to do just that and still comply with the terms of the agreement. He'd held her close during the tango display, wishing it would go on for ever so he could feel her close to him.

He knew he wasn't the only man who'd lusted after her tonight. He knew the look and he'd recognised it in other men's eyes. And just the thought of others thinking the same made his breath growl in his throat. He needed them to know she was his—truly his.

His eyes scanned the ballroom.

So why had he agreed to this no-sex rule? What was the point of it? Forced contraception? They could easily prevent an unwanted pregnancy—people did it all the time.

No, she'd turned up on his doorstep looking like a stray—no wonder he'd agreed to her no sex condition. But that was then.

Now he could see what she'd been hiding under her too big clothes. Now he wanted to see more.

And it wasn't enough to marry her. He needed to stamp her with his ownership so that everyone would know, without a shadow of a doubt, that she was his in every sense of the word.

She would agree.

There was no question she would agree.

Because he'd make sure she had no choice.

He caught sight of a familiar flash of colour across the room, heard a familiar laugh and saw greedy eyes turn his way, lighting up when they saw he was alone.

Yes, he looked forward to the coming contract renegotiations with another woman, but first he had a job to do.

CHAPTER SEVEN

THE DRESS WAS definitely the problem. Alesander watched her entertaining her circle of admirers and thought he should have let her choose one of the other gowns, as spectacular as they had been. But they had been nothing in comparison with this one, that turned woman into siren, hinting at what lay beneath if one was only reckless enough to try.

He was reckless enough to try.

Maybe if Ezmerelda had worn this dress tonight, nobody would have noticed Simone.

Then she laughed at something Markel had said and he saw the sparkle in her eyes and the warmth in her smile and he knew the dress would have made no difference. It was Simone who made the difference. Maybe the dress caught people's eye, but it was Simone herself who held their attention. The trouble was, there were too many people taking notice.

Correction—there were too many men.

He'd left her for what? All of fifteen minutes and yet now she was surrounded by them, Markel still there in the midst of them, no doubt wishing he was thirty years younger.

And he knew why they were there.

Because she was beautiful and desirable and they all thought she was his latest plaything and they were lining up for a piece of her when he was done.

And it was his fault. Because he'd never before been seen with a woman on his arm who he wasn't sleeping with and meaning to dispose of. He'd never before been seen with a woman who wasn't temporary.

He swallowed back on the bitter taste of bile at the back of his throat. Well, this woman might be temporary but he wasn't sleeping with her.

Not yet.

But he'd soon fix that.

He made his way across the room towards

them, knowing it was right to have decided what he had, already anticipating the pleasures that were to come. Finding a smile came easily, so easily in fact that she looked up at him and frowned and he realised he'd already forgotten about his little chat with Ezmerelda.

That made his smile widen even further.

Anticipation was a fine thing.

There must have been something in his eyes, for the other men drifted away, back to their own women, leaving only Markel, who snagged his arm as soon as he came close. 'You are a lucky man, Alesander. Simone is not only a beautiful woman, but she is clever and entertaining. Promise me you will not deprive us of her company in the future.'

'You're in luck, Markel, as it happens,' he said, sliding a proprietorial arm around Simone, who looked more confused than ever. 'I wasn't going to say anything—it is your birthday celebration after all, but there will be another party very soon and one to which you're invited, because a little earlier tonight Simone agreed to become my wife.'

'Your wife?' Markel blinked his surprise. 'But this is wonderful news!'

'I hoped you'd think so. I know Isobel and your wife had other plans.'

Markel waved the younger man's concerns away before laying his hand on Alesander's shoulder. 'As much as I would love to have you as my son-in-law, it was clear to me it was never going to happen. There was never any spark between you two. I tried to tell Ezmerelda that.' He shrugged. 'She chose not to listen. Her mother had put all kinds of fanciful notions into her head and she preferred to believe those.'

'I've already spoken to her tonight to let her know before she heard via other means.'

'*Bueno*. That was thoughtful of you.' Markel sighed wistfully. 'And perhaps it is good you are getting married because now she will forget her foolish dreams and finally see that there are other men in the world. I can only hope.

'As for you two,' he said, taking both their

hands in his meaty hand, 'I wish you every success and many, many fine sons.'

'How did Ezmerelda take it?' she asked when they were in the car and heading towards Getaria. 'Was it rough?'

He changed gears to take a bend, the car sticking to the road like glue. 'She cried.'

'Oh.'

'And then she pleaded.'

'Ah.'

'And then she wished us all the best in our married life.' He didn't tell her the rest, that she'd said she'd noticed they had a connection from the moment she'd seen them together and that was why she'd followed Simone to warn her off, because she'd never before felt so threatened. There were some things that sat uncomfortably with him. There were some things that Simone didn't need to know.

'That was nice of her, in the circumstances.'

'*Sí*, but it was good of you to think of telling her. That would not have occurred to me. It shows a generous spirit.'

She laughed at that. 'I don't know about that. I just wish we didn't have to deceive everyone this way. I never thought it would be so complicated. I was thinking only of Felipe when I came up with this plan and I never realised other people might get hurt by it. Like Markel. He's a nice man. I like him.'

'Markel is a good man.'

'I'm truly sorry he's going to be disappointed.'

'You mean because of the marriage ending?'

'Yes.' She sighed. 'But also because of all those fine sons you're not going to have.'

He smiled. He was in too good a mood not to. Tomorrow he would ask Felipe for Simone's hand in marriage. He didn't expect the old man to be happy about it, but he'd come around, just as soon as he realised it would mean the Otxoa family fortunes finally shifting in the right direction.

And then, as soon as he'd secured his agreement, he'd tell Simone he was changing the terms. She might not like it—no, more like it, she would hate it—but by then it would be too late.

And she would be his, in every sense of the word.

'What's the rush?' demanded Felipe at lunch the next day. 'You barely know each other.'

The three of them were sitting outside, the table set under an ancient pergola creaking under the weight of overgrown vines, sunlight filtering through the dense forest of leaves while far below them the sunlight turned the sea sparkling. Alesander had come over ostensibly to do some more work on the vines when she'd lured Felipe outside to enjoy the mild weather while it lasted. Over lunch, after they'd shared a bottle of last season's Txakolina wine that she was beginning to acquire a taste for, Felipe pouring it from a great height into tumblers to give life to the bubbles and clearly enjoying himself. And after lunch Alesander had asked Felipe for permission to marry her.

'Sometimes you just know, Abuelo.' Simone had expected the request to come as a shock and it had. Felipe's initial prejudices towards Alesander were softening each and every time he visited, she could tell, but there were still too many decades of rivalry between the neighbouring families to be calmly put aside.

'But marriage? Already?'

'It's not so soon. It will still take a month for the paperwork to be processed. The wedding won't take place until after harvest.'

He frowned. 'Do you love her?' he asked Alesander pointedly.

Simone winced. More lies, she thought, hating it. How many lies would they have to tell before this was over?

Except Alesander seemed unfazed. He took her hand in his, covering it with his other, while his eyes held hers, dark and rich and so deep a person could drown in their depths. 'I admit, I did not expect this to happen. But Simone blew into my life and how could I not love her, Felipe?

She is very special. One of a kind. How could I let her slip through my fingers?'

There was no stopping the bloom of heat in her cheeks. She smiled, deeply touched that he would take the trouble to find the words to put Felipe at his ease.

'I thought you wanted the vines,' he said, and there was a tear in his eye. 'I thought you were looking to take the rest of them away from me. But it is my granddaughter who brings you here day after day.'

Alesander looked at his feet and Simone knew she had to fill the silence. 'We want you to be there at our wedding, Abuelo. I was hoping you would agree to give me away.'

Her grandfather puffed up before her eyes, blinking away the moisture. 'And you think I won't be there to walk my only granddaughter down the aisle on her wedding day? Of course I will be there.'

He lifted his empty tumbler in his bony claw-like hand. 'More wine,' he demanded. 'This calls for a toast!'

* * *

'Thank you for that.'

She'd walked Alesander to his car, their lunch over, Felipe snoozing under the vine covered canopy.

'For what?'

'For putting Felipe's mind at ease about us getting married. When he asked you if you loved me, I thought the game was up.'

He cocked one eyebrow, one side of his mouth turned up. 'You imagined I would simply say no?'

'I didn't know what you would say.'

He took her hands in his and she thought nothing of it, given they were still in sight of the house if Felipe happened to wake up and see them. Besides, she was getting to like the feeling of him touching her. If only because that meant she was getting used to it and that made the pretence easier to pull off. 'It was not hard to think of words I could say about you. It is true you are one of a kind, and you definitely blew into my life by turning up on my doorstep with your crazy proposal. And how could I let you slip through my fingers when you had such a juicy incentive?' He paused and looked out over the sparkling sea. 'Felipe was right all along about that.'

'He doesn't think so now.'

'No. And hopefully he will never find out.'

'I know. I feel bad about the lies. But it's worth it. You can see how happy this has made him. For the first time he has something to look forward to. He's smiling again. Thank you so much for not only agreeing to this, but for actually going to the trouble of making him believe it.'

He looked back at her and smiled, squeezing her hands to tug her a little closer as he dipped his head towards hers. She held her breath as his mouth came closer; held her breath as she wondered whether he would kiss her—and whether she should let him—it wouldn't mean anything after all, just a token gesture and probably meant for Felipe's benefit in case he was watching and so why should she stop him?

And then he kissed her forehead and breath rushed out of her on a whoosh.

From relief, she told herself. Not disappointment, despite that sudden inexplicable pang in her chest.

Except he didn't let her go. His lips lingered on her forehead, she felt his breath fan against her skin and he let one hand go, only to take her chin in his fingers as slowly he pulled away, tilting up her head at the same time.

Her eyes met his and held. 'I have to kiss you,' he said, 'but properly this time and, I warn you, it may take some time.'

'For Felipe's benefit?' she managed to say. 'In case he is watching.'

He growled, the corners of his mouth turning up the tiniest fraction. 'For my benefit.'

If such a confession wasn't enough to make her senses sing, the sensation of his lips meshing with hers was. Her breath hitched again at their impact, before she was assailed by the feel of his mouth against hers and the sheer complexity of it all—the unexpected contrast of lips that felt so warm and yielding and yet came from a face that could have been sculpted from stone. And the way he tasted…a heated blend of the wine they'd shared at lunch with coffee and all overlaid on the flavour of his own hot mouth.

He was addictive.

He was incendiary.

Her heart rate kicked up as she felt his hand draw her closer and she let herself be drawn as his tongue searched out hers and invited it into a dance—a dance that soon turned into a heated frenzy that had her temperature soaring and her heart beating even faster and her flesh throbbing in secret places situated a long way geographically from her mouth.

If the man knew nothing else, he sure knew how to kiss. Every place they touched seemed hyper-aware—her breasts jammed close to his chest, her hips hard against his thighs, her legs interwoven with his.

It was far more than any kiss she'd ever experienced.

And it was the last thing she'd wanted, but right now it made it too damned good to leave.

Instead it was Alesander who pulled away suddenly, putting her at arm's length, leaving her mouth hungry and desperately seeking his. Desperately seeking more. He was breathing hard, but she was breathing harder, and struggling hard to show she was not as affected as she was.

Failing miserably.

'We need to plan,' he said, his breathing choppy and desperate against her face. 'Are you taking precautions?'

For a kiss? Now she had to struggle with the meaning behind his words. She wasn't sure she'd heard right. 'Excuse me?'

'Are you on the Pill? Do you call it that where you come from—the contraceptive pill?'

She eased away. Even managed to laugh a little, while she put distance between them, though nowhere near enough to let him go completely. She wasn't ready for that yet and, besides, he was showing no intention of letting her go any time soon. 'What business is that of yours?'

'Because we will need precautions.'

'Against—what exactly? We've agreed we're not having sex. Why would we need precautions?'

'Because I've changed my mind. I'm not marrying you and not having sex with you.'

This time she found the strength to shove him away. 'No! You signed a contract! We both signed a contract. We agreed there would be no sex.'

'And I'm renegotiating the terms.'

'You can't do that. It's too late.'

'Of course I can. I don't like the terms and I'm changing them.'

'And I refuse to agree to your changed terms. There will be no sex in our marriage.'

'And I say there will.'

'What? And you think you can make me? I don't think so. I'm not changing anything. I don't want it.'

'Are you sure of that? I just got the impression you would quite happily have had me, right here, right up against the car next to the vines if I hadn't stopped, and you would have let me.'

Shock forced her jaw wide open. 'You imagine this because I let you kiss me just now?'

'You did more than let me kiss you. Your body told me it wanted me.'

'You flatter yourself,' she said, shaking her head, in denial because she had to be. He had felt good, it was true. Maybe very good. But he could not know what she had been thinking. 'You're wrong. I don't want you. Sure, we shared a kiss, and maybe it was okay, but it was only for Felipe's benefit.'

'Now who's kidding themselves? You weren't thinking about Felipe when I kissed you.'

'That doesn't mean we're having sex. There's no way I want sex with you. No way at all.'

'Fine.' He took a step back from her. 'I must have been mistaken. If that's the way you want it, I will go back up there and tell Felipe this marriage is off.'

'What? Why? I don't understand. You make one arrangement and then you insist on another?

You can't do that to him! How could you do that after everything we've done? Felipe believes it now. He believes we're getting married. He thinks he's walking me down the aisle. How could you do this to him?'

'How could I do that to him?' he said. 'No. You should be asking how *you* could do this to him. You're the one suddenly wanting to deny him his happy ending.'

He was shifting the blame onto her? 'I can't believe you're doing this. Though maybe I should, because Felipe warned me from the very start that I should be careful. He said you were an Esquivel and that I shouldn't trust you, that you would be ruthless. I should have listened to him all along.'

'Maybe you should have.'

His cold, hard words floored her. Where was the man who had sucked her into his kiss, and whose heat had damned near melted her flesh? Where was that man? Had he been an entire fiction? She felt sick just thinking about how much she'd wanted him. 'I hate you. I don't think I've ever hated you more than in this moment.'

'That's fine. I told you I wasn't nice. Hating me will make it so much easier when you leave.'

CHAPTER EIGHT

SHE WANTED TO hate him after that. She did her best to. Late at night atop her single bed she did all she could to hate him. But hate disappeared in the overwhelming truth.

She should never have let him kiss her.

Now her body ached to make love to him and yet she didn't want to make love to him. She couldn't make love to him. Making love made a person vulnerable. She'd learned that with Damon, their relationship going from boyfriend and girlfriend, moving with their lovemaking to a higher level. To love. Or so she'd thought.

Damon's betrayal had ripped all sense of wanting intimacy out of her. Keep it platonic, she'd learned. Keep it simple, and you couldn't be hurt.

Keep it platonic—businesslike—and there could be no complications.

She knew this to be true. She knew she'd been right to insist on a sex-free marriage. She didn't want to go through what she had with Damon again. She couldn't live with the fear and the gut-sickening uncertainty.

And yet still the thought of Alesander's threatened lovemaking left her breathless and hungry. She tossed and turned in the small bed, tangling in the sheets, thinking about sheets tangled for other, more carnal, reasons.

Wishing that she didn't look forward to it as much as she dreaded it.

Wishing she could simply hate him and be done with it.

She tossed again. Oh God, why the hell couldn't she sleep?

The season shifted inexorably towards the harvest, and Alesander was busier, managing both his own business and yet still finding time to spend in Felipe's vineyard, repairing trellises and filling in pot-holes in the driveway and, even though she knew he was doing it because the land would soon be his, she could not hate him for it when she saw how it made Felipe happier, to see his vines and the vineyard looking cared for again.

She tried to keep her distance as much as she could but somehow he was always there, shrinking the tiny cottage with his presence, talking to Felipe about the grapes, or comparing techniques to manage the vines.

And there could be no avoiding him because, as the harvest drew closer, so too did their wedding. Alesander appointed a wedding planner charged with the task of organising a wedding extravaganza in less than a month. Simone was happy to leave her to it, but there was no escaping the endless questions. There were meetings to be had, decisions to be made, plans to be drawn up.

And nothing could wait. Every little thing was urgent.

'I can't get a church,' the wedding planner admitted at one of their first meetings, looking harried and stressed. 'You've waited too long. San

Sebastian's churches are booked up months in advance and the village churches are full.'

Alesander brushed the problem aside. 'Then we'll get married in the Esquivel vineyard. It's unconventional, but everyone will understand.'

The wedding planner looked noticeably relieved and turned to Simone. 'Have you decided on who will be your attendant?'

Simone blinked. 'Do I really need one?'

The planner looked askance at Alesander. 'Who have you chosen as your best man?'

'A friend from Madrid. Matteo Cachon.'

Simone's ears pricked up. The name sounded vaguely familiar.

'Not the football player?' asked the woman, and Simone realised where she'd heard it. On the evening news. Matteo Cachon had just been signed in a massive deal that made him Spain's most valuable football player. In the same report came the news he'd just dumped his long-term girlfriend, so he was also Spain's most eligible bachelor.

He nodded. '*Sí.* He's an old friend from university. We don't see each other much these days but it fits in his schedule and he's agreed.'

'I have an idea about an attendant,' Simone said, and when the wedding planner looked expectantly back at her, pen poised, added, 'I'll ask her and get back to you.'

Meanwhile Felipe was the happiest she'd ever seen him. He seemed to have dropped twenty years overnight. He even seemed to have more energy, demanding to be taken into town to be fitted out with a brand new suit, his first new suit since his marriage to Maria more than fifty years before.

It made it all worthwhile, even after the visit to his doctor, who'd taken her aside while Felipe was getting dressed to warn that while Felipe was feeling happier, she shouldn't make the mistake of thinking he was getting better. There would be no getting better.

She'd thanked the doctor and swallowed back on a bubble of disappointment. Deep down inside she'd known that to be true, that there would be no sudden miracle or remission. She just hadn't wanted to give that knowledge oxygen.

But the doctor's warning made up her mind. She would stop this Cold War approach to Alesander. She would stop trying to make herself hate him and instead try to make this marriage look as happy for Felipe as she possibly could, although she hated the changed terms.

Because she would not let Felipe down.

The grapes tested perfectly one crisp day early in October and from then on it was madness. Swarms of workers filled the Esquivel vineyards, filling boxes with bunches of grapes, boxes emptied into a tractor drawn behind a trailer to be taken straight to the press.

Simone worked in Felipe's vineyard as part of a team sent by Alesander, wearing oversized gloves and with a pair of thin-bladed snippers, perfectly designed for separating the bunches from the vines. If you knew what you were doing. In no time she knew she was the slowest person on the team. But she was determined to catch on, filling box after box with bunches of grapes.

Felipe sat on the vine-covered terrace and kept an eye on the progress, muttering to himself.

They took a break halfway through the morning, sitting amidst the vines, talking and laughing amongst themselves while they shared the most magnificent view on earth, and Simone felt privileged to experience this; to be part of something so utterly unique that she would never share in again. It made her sorry that she would ever have to leave.

And then they were back at work and there was no time for regret, only time for the grapes.

Alesander turned up at lunch time, with platters of food from a local restaurant, which the pickers shared around a big trestle table set up for the job.

'Thank you for this,' she told him near the car when he was leaving, and it didn't matter this time whether she thought he was being nice or not, or whether she thought he was only doing it because he would soon own these vines, because she appreciated the gesture just the same. 'Thank you for so much.'

He scooped her into his arms and dipped his head down and kissed her lightly on the lips, to the delight of everyone at the table nearby. 'I've missed you,' he said, and she knew he meant how she'd held herself separate from him while she'd told herself she hated him.

Because, in spite of all her reservations, she'd missed him too.

'We get married in three days,' he said.

'Do you think the harvest will be finished?'

He growled and she felt it reverberate through her bones while his eyes held her hostage. 'I don't care. I'm marrying you anyway.' And then he kissed her again.

It was because they were all watching, she told herself, as she snipped grapes for the next day and a half. He'd only said it because people were watching.

But still, regardless of what he'd meant, or whatever his motivation, she'd cherish forever the look in his eyes when he'd uttered those words.

Three mornings later, the harvest completed, she donned the dress that would make her the

Esquivel bride. Her gown was by the same designer as the one she'd worn to Markel's birthday party. Alesander had insisted on it and she'd argued that it wasn't necessary, right up until she'd seen the gown paraded before them and wished it could be hers and before she'd had a chance to say she loved it, he'd said, 'That one,' and she'd known they were both right even before she'd tried it on.

And it was perfect. With its fitted bodice and tight waist and pleating across her hips, it echoed in so many ways the gown she'd worn to Markel's party, but then this gown was so much more, the layers filmy and soft and the perfect foil to the fitted bodice.

Simone didn't have to ask how she looked. Today there was no joking. Tears sprang from her grandfather's eyes as she emerged from her room—tears that said it all. Tears that made all the lies she'd told suddenly worthwhile. It was worth it, she told herself, to see how happy Felipe looked today.

It was all worth it.

'You look beautiful,' he said in his thready voice. 'You have made me the proudest man in the world.'

'And you look wonderful, too.' And he did, freshly shaved and in his new suit. She worried about his role, walking her down the aisle, and wondered if he was up to it, but today he looked ready for anything.

'Come on,' he said, offering her his arm, 'the car is waiting for us.'

They arrived at the Esquivel vineyard to find most of the village waiting expectantly for her outside the vaulted cellars where the wedding was to take place.

'Don't be worried,' her attendant said from the front seat. 'Celebrations always follow the harvest. This is just one more cause for celebration.'

It was, apparently, as cameras clicked and buzzed around her as the bridal party made it from the car. Felipe took the longest time, untangling his legs but still smiling as he took his granddaughter's arm for the walk down the short aisle.

Ezmerelda set off first, serene and magnificent and so calm it lent Simone strength. She followed on Felipe's arm, his steps faltering and slow, but he beamed proudly to everyone along the way.

This is his moment, she thought, much more than mine, and she slowed her steps to match his, and let him have his moment. He was back, celebrating with the people he'd lived with all his life, the people he'd been cut off from, first with his wife's illness and then with his own disease.

He was in his element and he was lapping it up.

And then she saw Alesander waiting for her.

So tall and broad, and so breathtakingly handsome beyond belief, and smiling indulgently, as if he knew what she was doing taking so long making her way down the aisle.

His smile worked its way into her bones. No wonder it was so hard to tell herself she should hate him.

Finally they were there and she kissed Felipe

on the cheeks as he left her with her husband-to-be. She'd done it, she thought as she listened to her vows. Her crazy plan had worked out.

Or almost worked out.

And minutes later, as they were declared man and wife and they kissed, now it was almost done. Now there was just the reception and Alesander's contract amendments to work through…

The reception was the easy bit. Ezmerelda was right, the village was in the mood to celebrate, and Felipe was not missing out on anything. She saw him stagger his way onto the dance floor as Alesander whirled her around the floor, and she wondered how long his strength would last, but how could she stop him when he was having so much fun?

Alesander whisked her past. 'However did you do it?' he asked. 'However did you get Ezmerelda on side to be your attendant?'

She smiled and looked across to the couple who had danced non-stop since the music had started, the couple the photographers were almost one hundred per cent focused upon. 'All I had to do was tell her I knew nothing about weddings and I needed her help.'

'That's all?'

'Okay, it did help when I mentioned who your best man was.'

He laughed. 'You are an amazing woman, Señora Esquivel.'

She blinked up at him and wished things could be different. 'And you are an amazing man.'

He pulled her to him and they shared that moment as he spun her around the dance floor, and this time she let herself relax and be held because it felt so good when this man held her and she knew it wouldn't last.

It didn't last. Barely a minute into the dance they heard the cries of panic.

It only took a second to work out why the music and dancing had stopped.

Felipe had collapsed on the dance floor.

CHAPTER NINE

'YOU SEEM tense,' Alesander said, as the car cruised through the quiet streets, his arm wound around her shoulders, his warm fingers tracing patterns on her skin.

'Do I?' She wasn't really surprised. She'd thought she was relaxed when they'd left the hospital. She'd accepted his arm around her shoulders and let herself tap into his strength, but on reflection she hadn't been relaxed at all. She'd just been relieved—that Felipe, in his weakened state, had simply overdone things and would be released after a night's observation. But the relief hadn't lasted long. Because almost as soon as the car had left the hospital she'd realised where they were headed.

To Alesander's apartment.

To Alesander's bed.

And the relief at knowing Felipe was in good

hands for the night was no match for the apprehension that had followed. The pressure of his arm around her shoulders—the stroke of his fingers across her skin—the press of his strong thigh against hers—all of these sensations only served to ratchet up her tension and heighten her anxiety.

Because he had decreed that in spite of the agreement they'd both signed—the agreement that stipulated that this was a marriage in name only—that he intended to exercise all of his marital rights and bed her.

No, she thought on reflection, not decreed. Because this man had blackmailed her to make it so.

The fact he'd waited until their wedding night for it to happen didn't help at all.

Not now that night was here.

'The doctors say Felipe will be all right,' he said beside her, squeezing her shoulder, trying to reassure her, misinterpreting her nervousness. And that only made her angrier. Because this marriage was a device—a convenience—

nothing more. Alesander didn't know the first thing about her. He didn't know what made her tick. He had no concept of what was troubling her like a man who loved her—like a real husband—would.

And yet he was expecting to take her to his bed and share the ultimate intimacy, as if he were that real husband—as if he actually cared about her.

Damn him! They'd made an agreement. They'd both signed it, only for him to go and change the rules mid-play, and all because he couldn't handle the thought of a woman who wasn't interested in him, who didn't throw herself at his feet as he was used to.

'That must be a disappointment for you,' she countered, shifting herself as far as she could along the seat, wanting to put distance between them, or at least distance between their warm thighs, 'or it might have been the shortest wedding in history. You could already have been halfway to owning the entire vineyard.'

Something hard and sharp glinted in his eyes

as they met hers. 'I guess we are stuck together a little longer, in that case. And as much as that might bother you and inconvenience us both, luckily there is a silver lining attached to every dark cloud.'

She gave an unladylike snort. 'Really? So name it.'

'That's easy,' he said as he smiled and touched his hand to her forehead, where the ends of a stray curl had tangled in her lashes. With an all too gentle swipe of his fingers against her brow, he pulled the offending curl free. She shivered under the touch of his fingertip on her skin, and at the tug of hair against lash. She shivered again when she realised how much his touch affected her and how very much she didn't want it to. 'Because I get to make love to you, of course. What else could it be?'

And if she didn't already harbour enough resentment towards this man, she could hate him for the smug certainty that tonight it would happen. That tonight they would make love.

And even as he sought to relax her with the

touch of his hand and the stroke of his fingers across her skin, instead his hand felt like the weight of obligation on her shoulders, his fingers heavy at the expectation of what this wedding night should bring.

A wedding night that should never be.

It was all so wrong.

It was all so false.

She looked out of the window, silently fuming, breathing deep, pretending interest in the buildings of the Platje de la Concha rather than look anywhere near him—at this man who was now her husband in name and who very shortly intended to make himself her husband in every intimate sense of the word.

And yet still not a husband at all. A real husband would marry you because he loved you. Because he wanted to be with you and wanted to spend the rest of his life with you.

Not just because he thought he could get the vines you would inherit and get into your pants in the same deal.

'Stop the car,' she vaguely registered hearing,

confused when they were still blocks away from his apartment.

The driver pulled in along the kerb. 'What are you doing?' she asked as he stepped from the car and held out his hand to her.

'Making an executive decision,' he said, his smile at odds with his tight features. 'It's such a beautiful night I thought we might both benefit from a walk along the beach.'

She looked up at him, searching his eyes in the night light, searching for meaning or another, darker, motive, but she could find none. And while it was a relief to know he wasn't so desperate to get her on her back that he would head straight to his apartment, it was disturbing too, that perhaps he wasn't as oblivious of her feelings as she had assumed. 'Thank you,' she simply said, because a walk along the beach suited her too, if only because it gave her much needed breathing space. She slid across the seat and took his hand to join him in the dark night air. 'I would appreciate that.'

The car pulled away, the driver dismissed,

as Alesander tucked her arm into his and led her along the wide lamplit walkway. The mild night air kissed her skin, whispering in its salty tongue, while a fat moon hung low, sending a ribbon of silver across the water. From somewhere came the sounds of music, the strains of a violin to which the low waves whooshed in and out along the shore. Beside her Alesander said little, seemingly content also to absorb the evening, their war of words and wills temporarily suspended.

He was right, she thought, as they strolled their slow way around the bay. It was a beautiful night, a night made for lovers, a night where the air held a note of expectation, almost as if it was holding its breath waiting for something. And that thought left her sad, that this night and all its romance was wasted on them. Because she had no expectations. Hers was an obligation. Hers was nothing to look forward to.

Although...

She stole a look at his strong profile. His was not a face you would be disappointed waking up to after the night before. His body was not one you would regret reaching out for. And then she shivered a little, turning her eyes back to the path and trying not to think too much about that night before.

The night to come.

Was she pathetic to feel so nervous? She'd got naked with a man. She'd had sex. She knew how it worked and where the various bits went. Sometimes she'd even enjoyed it. But that had been with Damon, and they'd been a couple for almost a year. She'd even imagined she loved him at one stage—before she'd found out he was happily having sex with her best friend behind her back. But they'd been friends before they'd become lovers. Of course there had been times it had been good with him.

But sex with a virtual stranger?

Sex with a man who had blackmailed her into his bed?

There was no way she could enjoy that.

And there was no way she could trust her feelings when she did. Intimacy came with a price, one she wasn't sure she wanted to pay again.

'Are you cold?' he asked, as if he'd sensed her tremor.

'I'm fine,' she replied, wishing he hadn't noticed, not wanting him to know anything about her, uncomfortable with the thought he was reading her body.

'Then why don't we walk on the beach?'

'Take our shoes off, you mean?'

'Unless you can walk in high heels on the sand.' And his smile caught the moonlight and his teeth glinted white to match the spark in his eyes and the idea was so unexpected that she laughed.

'Why not?'

She slipped off her silver sandals and unhooked the stockings from her suspenders, slipping them down her legs while he shrugged off his shoes before taking her hand. The sand was cool under her feet and tickled the sensitive skin between her toes. His hand was warm, his long fingers curled around hers, his thumb drawing lazy circles on her wrist.

She tried to concentrate on the sand and the squeak of their steps on the sand, on the lights of the buildings reflected into the bay, on the stars and moon above, but his touch wasn't easy to ignore. Damon hadn't liked holding hands. He'd said it signalled possessiveness and argued that people weren't possessions.

Was Alesander being possessive or just… neighbourly? Whatever, he had nice hands and a nice touch. She didn't mind the feel of her hand wrapped in his as they walked along the sand. And meanwhile the silver ribbon on the water shimmied, the shoreline spun with gold of the reflected city and the night air was fresh and clean.

She sighed wistfully. 'It's so beautiful here. You're lucky to live so close to the bay.'

'Do you live near the sea?'

'No, not really. I live in a shoe box of a flat near the university where I'm studying. It's about an hour to the coast, probably two to get to a de-cent beach.' She sighed again. 'The beach there is nice enough but it's nothing like this.'

They walked a few more steps, the strains of the violin haunting in the night air.

'What are you studying?'

And the question took her so unawares that she laughed.

'What's so funny?'

She shook her head. 'I don't know. It just seemed odd—we just got married and here you are, asking me what I do. Normally you'd ask that before you got married.'

'Normally a woman wouldn't turn up on your doorstep and propose.'

'Yeah,' she said, looking at her feet. 'I take your point. I'm studying psychology. I'm in my final year.'

They neared a building that jutted out onto the beach—the same restaurant near where she'd crossed the road that first day—which meant his apartment must be just across the road. Here the music was louder, and she could see a small band of musicians playing on a balcony overlooking the sea, scattered patrons lapping up the last of the evening's musical fare. The music tugged at her as they passed by, the violin so sweet over the piano and drums, so richly emotional that she stopped to listen. 'What is that tune?'

'That one?' He smiled. 'It's an old folk song. The lyrics tell of the mountains and the sea and the people who settled here originally and made it home. But most times they don't bother with the lyrics. They let the violin sing the words.'

'It's so beautiful,' she said as she watched the violinist coax his instrument to even sweeter heights.

For a moment it was just the music and the tide that filled the space between and all around them, until he uttered the words, 'You are,' and she felt the night air shift sensually around her. 'Very beautiful.'

She looked back up at him, startled, to see him smiling down at her, and maybe it was the music that she could hear, the music that sounded so poignant and bewitching against the rhythmic shush of the tide, or maybe it was the velvet sky and the silver ribbon of moonlight on the water, but she caught the spine-tingling impact of his smile full on and then immediately wished she hadn't. Because she didn't want him to smile at her like that. She didn't want him to smile at her at all. She didn't want him to tell her she was beautiful and make out this marriage was something more than it was.

And suddenly she regretted letting him take her hand and walk her along the sand as if they were friends or even lovers. They were neither. They had a business arrangement, that was all it was, the terms of which he'd changed to suit himself, and only after it was too late for her to get out of it, once she was already committed. And now this whole 'walk on the sands holding hands' episode spoke of nothing more than lulling her into some false sense of security— to make her think he actually cared—when his apartment was right across the street and it was clear that was where they were headed next—so he could finish this thing he'd started.

She wasn't having it. She shook her head,

saying no to whatever it was he was offering, vaguely aware of another tune, violin over drumbeat, half familiar.

Momentarily it threw her. Until she realised it was the music that had played at Markel's birthday party, the tango to which the dancers had danced so seductively. So passionately.

The music he'd told her was called *Feelings*.

And the music told her what a marriage should be. The music told her what was missing from this marriage and could never be a part of it.

Emotion.

Powerful, strong emotion.

It was the final straw.

'I'm sorry. I can't do this any more.'

'You cannot walk along the beach?'

She wanted to lash out at him. Did he deliberately go out of his way to misunderstand her? Surely it was obvious? 'The moon. The beach. Holding hands. All of it. I don't want it. I cannot pretend to be some blushing bride. I cannot look forward to a wedding night that I wanted no part of, that you have blackmailed me into.'

'Is it such a dire prospect that you face, making love with me?'

'When it was unwanted all along? When it remains so? Of course it is!'

'Unwanted?'

'Haven't I made that clear from the start?'

He paused a moment, looking into space, almost as if listening to the building music, the evocative violin, before he looked back at her. 'You're the one who agreed to change the terms.'

'Only because you threatened to tell Felipe our marriage was a sham! Do you know how much I hate you for that? You left me with no choice and then you have the gall to think I will happily fall into bed with you! I cannot believe how arrogant you are. You are everything I hate in a man and nothing I want in a husband!'

She finished her tirade breathless and panting and mentally preparing herself for his next shot, expecting to receive the full force of his fury.

'Dance with me,' he said instead.

'What?'

His flashing eyes sent out a challenge as the

instruments merged, their sound weaving together on the night air. He took a purposeful
step. Or more a glide across the sand. And then
another, his body straight, his head held high.
'Dance with me.'

'No. It's too crazy. I don't know how.'

'You do,' he told her, changing direction. 'You
are doing it now, with your tongue. With your
words. Do it instead with your body. Show me
how angry you are.'

'No!' she insisted, turning away, the idea of
dancing with this man on the beach too ridiculous to consider. 'There is no point.'

But she'd barely taken a step before he'd
grabbed her wrist and spun her bodily back into
him, her shoes and stockings flung far from her
grip. She collided bodily against his chest, her
hands between them, the air knocked from her
lungs and angry as hell at being plastered full
length against him.

'I said no!' She shoved hard against his chest
and wheeled away but he had hold of her hand

and she was at arm's length again before he snapped her breathlessly back into his embrace.

'You bastard!' With her hands at his shoulders, she pushed herself away as far as she could, but his arms were wound around her waist, his eyes intent on hers, and she could do nothing as he moved in a circle around her, his body as tight, his movements as purposeful as the dancer they'd seen. 'What the hell do you think you're doing?'

'I am dancing. With my wife. Do you have a problem with that?'

'Yes!' When it meant his hands were like steel bands around her and his muscled chest like a wall under her hands. She'd seen that chest naked and in all its glory and now her fingers drank in every detail of the feel of him. He was so hard and lean and magnificent and she wanted to be nowhere near him because she didn't want her hands to tell her these things.

'I can't dance. Not this.'

'You will find it easier if you put your arms around my neck.'

Easier? Perhaps, but at least her hands wouldn't be subjected to the play of muscle under skin. Her grip relaxed, her hands sliding their way around his neck. He growled, a low sound of appreciation that rumbled its way into her bones as he spun her in a circle around him.

And then he slid one hand up behind his neck and took one of her hands in his own, drawing it down to his mouth to kiss the palm of her hand. She gasped, the sensation of his tongue flicking across the sensitive skin, the look of his eyes so darkly intent on hers, the music made for couples, the feel of his arm wrapped tightly around her waist—it was too much.

He took one slow step, and then another, drawing her across the sand. Long purposeful steps. Powerful. Dramatic. He guided her back, leading her with his touch and his body before he spun her around and dropped her low over his arm, holding her so securely that even for one so inexperienced she was never in any danger of falling. 'You see,' he said, drawing her slowly up again, held tight against his body, setting up a delicious friction in her breasts and her belly and the aching place between her thighs, 'you can do this.'

'I hate you,' she said, because she was enjoying it too much, this feel of him hard against her as they moved across the sand.

'That's what makes it so good,' he told her, turning her slowly in his embrace. 'Conflict and desire in one explosive package.'

'Who said anything about desire?'

He spun her then, her wedding gown spinning out in layers with her, and pulled her back first against his chest, his arms locking her so close she gasped when she felt the hard ridge of his arousal against her behind. Blatant. Shameless. *Arousing.*

And every muscle inside her contracted in response.

She should be outraged. She should demand to be let go. But instead heat pooled between her aching thighs, her breasts felt heavy and hard and it was all she could do not to squirm her bottom harder against him.

'Your body does, every time we touch.'

She shuddered, knowing there was no denying it but not wanting him to take any satisfaction from it. 'It doesn't mean anything. It doesn't mean I like you. It's purely a physical reaction.'

Behind her he laughed, the sound rippling through her flesh, his warm breath fanning her ear. 'Oh, I'm good with old-fashioned lust.'

And she realised the enormity of what she'd just admitted to, the admission she'd made. 'No!' she cried, fighting her way out of the prison of his arms, desperate to flee. He was too confident, too damned smug, too damned right. 'It doesn't mean—'

But once again she was no match for his speed and strength, no match for his determination. He caught both her wrists as she fled, snaring her back, plastering her against him, hip to hip, chest to chest, his face just inches from her own as his fingers curled through her hair.

'It means you want me.'

'No.'

'And I want you.'

'No.' But this time her voice was more a plea than a protest.

He smiled then, his eyes locked with hers, his thumb stroking her parted lips. 'What does it take, I wonder, to make you say yes?'

'Never,' she breathed, knowing it would do no good, her eyes already locked on the mouth hovering over hers, already contemplating his coming kiss, anticipating it, already tasting him.

Even so, when his kiss came, when his fingers tangled in her hair and his mouth meshed with hers, still she was unprepared for the maelstrom that followed, the storm that was unleashed inside her. Like a flooded river bursting its banks, her need spilled over, threatening to swamp her under the deluge.

She clung to him like a drowning person clung to a rock, as sensation ruled her world and threatened to sweep her away on the sensual tide of his taste and hot mouth and how he made her feel.

Desirable.

Desired.

Delicious.

He feasted on her and she let him, because that gave her licence to feast upon him, to taste his mouth and his salty skin, to relish the texture of his whiskered jaw as it rubbed against her cheek.

She clung to him because she did not want to let him go, now she had finally unleashed her hands on him and could drink in his perfect body through thirsting, seeking fingers.

She clung to him because she could not let him go and stop this thing now that it had started, this thing she had denied herself for so achingly, pointlessly long.

Her lips parted easily under the assault of his feasting mouth and tongue, her hands clinging to him as she opened to his kisses and passion became her master.

Passion, and the music she could still hear, the drumbeat that called to her on some primitive level and that guaranteed this moment was all important; that promised that this moment was pivotal to her entire existence.

She believed it as he swept her into his kiss, and swept any remaining logic away in the process. His breath was hot as his mouth slipped from her mouth to her throat and she gasped in the night air. His hands left hot trails on her back and she arched against him, no longer bothering to pretend it wasn't exactly where she wanted to be.

He was hot. So hot. And her need turned suddenly combustible, from flood into flame, threatening to consume her with its heated promise.

And pressed against him, her thigh between his, her belly against his hip, the rigid column of his erection promised more heat. Promised all she needed and more.

Much more.

She wanted it. She wanted him to fill her and to feel him deep inside her and that need was premier.

Despite his blackmail. Despite his smug certainty that it would happen.

And she learned something about herself then, in the scorching heat of his hot mouth and stroking tongue and seeking, inquisitive hands. She learned that she could tolerate blackmail, forgive arrogance and sweep aside the worst character faults, if this was to be her reward.

'I want you,' he said, wrenching himself breathlessly from his kiss, one hand curled around her breast, his fingers stroking over her nipple until it was achingly hard, his other hand sliding down to tantalisingly cup the curve of her behind. And his declaration was so raw and honest that even if his touch hadn't already been electric and set her senses on fire she could not deny it.

'I know,' she gasped.

'You want me,' he said, a statement rather than a question, and there was a challenge in his eyes, a challenge for her to give in and admit it and utter the word she could not say.

She did, but still she shook her head, if you could call the half-hearted movement a shake. 'It doesn't mean anything.'

'That's just the point,' he growled, low in his throat, hesitating just a moment before sucking her into the whirlpool of his kiss. 'It doesn't have to.'

CHAPTER TEN

IT SHOULD MEAN something. She wanted so much to disagree with him, she wanted to argue the case for the affirmative. Except with her body jammed tight up against his and his mouth locked on hers, his seeking tongue like an inferno to her senses, it was hard to think straight. It was hard to remember why it was so important.

And in the end logic got swept away by the tide of need. Making love with this man wasn't just a contract condition—an obligation. Making love with Alesander was as inevitable as the constant whoosh of the tide or the falling of the night or the rising of the moon. There was no stopping it. It was always going to happen.

She was in the lift before she realised they'd somehow crossed the road, barefoot and locked in each other's arms, lost in sensation. She was consumed with heat and him and a need that threatened to engulf her.

The lift was slow.

Alesander was faster.

He had her backed against the wall, one hand tangled in her hair, the other sweeping aside the layers of her skirt in a bid to reach her heated flesh. She gasped, the touch of his hand on her thigh searing, electric, and her body pulsed and ached and vaguely she thought that if the lift didn't hurry up he might just take her here and now.

His hand glided higher, his thumb skimmed her mound and a million nerve endings screamed inside her and she wished he damned well would.

But before he could the lift doors opened and they tumbled out together across the private lobby. He pulled off his jacket while he fumbled for the key, still locked in their kiss. His tie followed as the door opened and he put his hands to her shoulders and put her away from him, his dark eyes almost black with need, his breathing choppy. 'I was going to do this slowly,' he said, 'but I don't think I can wait that long.'

Her simmering blood rejoiced. She didn't want to wait. She couldn't. Now that she was on this course, now she had made her choice, she didn't want time to reflect or analyse or allow logic to intervene. There would be time for reflection later. Maybe even time for regret.

But that was later.

Right now she had other priorities.

'I don't want to wait either.'

And he growled as he swept her up into his arms and kicked the door closed behind them on his way to his bed.

If he noticed her weight in his arms, he didn't show it; he was so strong and powerful as he strode purposefully through the apartment, and she was nervous, her heart pounding, knowing and yet not knowing what was to come. She was no innocent. She'd had sex before and there had been times it had been good. Essentially it was the same act of intimacy. There was nothing new.

And yet something told her that this time was different.

Maybe because this time she was with a man, who made Damon seem like a boy in comparison.

Was it wrong of her to imagine just for a moment that this was real? Would it hurt to pretend, just for a little while, that she was a real bride and that this was a real wedding night?

His room shared the same magnificent view as the living room, the waters of the bay dark with a foaming white edge, framed by the lights of the city and the mountains that stood guard, and all frosted in silver from a lovers' moon.

Her view was better.

Dark-featured and olive-skinned, he was beautiful, this arrogant Spaniard, his hot mouth ripe for pleasure, his body built for sin.

He let her down slowly and set her on her bare feet without letting her go. Almost—she wanted to believe—almost, as if he couldn't bear to. His eyes locked with hers, dark eyes storm-tossed and brimming with need—*need for her*—and the knowledge was as precious as it was empowering.

When she was back home in her tiny flat in Melbourne, where San Sebastian and arrogant Spaniards and endless sunshine would be nothing but a distant memory, just knowing she'd had a man like Alesander wanting her would be something to pull out on a cold wintry night to warm her frigid bones.

His dark eyes burned for her. And she might be nothing to him, she knew, but she was the one with him here now. She was the one he wanted now.

His hands slipped over her shoulders and down the bare skin of her back. Hot. Seeking. She felt the slide of the zip and her strapless gown loosened around her. It was all she could do not to reach for it as it fell away from her breasts. It was all she could do to let the weight of her skirt drag the gown to the floor without trying to cover herself. Until it was too late to do anything and she stood nervously before him, naked but for a lace garter meant for stockings abandoned somewhere with her shoes upon the sand, and the tiny scrap of silk that was her underwear.

Breath hissed through his teeth as his eyes raked over her, her nipples hardening at the cool caress of air after being constrained by her tight bodice. Her breasts firming, her nipples peaking more with his heated gaze. 'Beautiful,' he murmured and she let the word sink in and float down like a leaf to some special place deep inside. He touched the pads of his fingers to her throat and like an echo she could feel her heartbeat in his touch. Their gazes locked as he followed the line of her collarbone to her shoulder. His touch was electric, torturous and yet simultaneously exquisite, too damned good to bear, too damned good to stop.

And when his knuckles drifted lower, her world waited, breathing hitched, her nipples aching to be touched, as his fingers skimmed the curve of her breast.

It was ecstasy.

It was agony.

'I thought you were in a hurry.' Her protesting

voice sounded thin and desperate and trembled like her knees.

'Forgive me,' he said. 'Do you know how perfect you are? I am in awe.'

She closed her eyes to stop the words getting in. In case she believed them. 'What you are,' she whispered shakily, 'is overdressed.'

He laughed, low and deep, that way he did, and her nipples peaked with pleasure. 'Don't they say patience is a virtue?'

'Virtue is overrated.'

He growled and she felt the jolt at her core. 'Is this what you want?' he asked, rolling her nipple between thumb and forefinger, teasing it mercilessly before he curled his fingers around her breast and squeezed tight.

She whimpered, her eyelids fluttering closed, and he took her hand before she knew what was happening. 'Or is this what you want?'

She gasped when she realised what he had planned. Gasped again at what she felt, the size of him, the strength, and it was her turn to be awed.

Awed, and grateful too, because she knew she could not have been so bold and he had given her licence.

He shrugged off his shirt as she tested his length in her fingers. He was so big. Long. Thick. She felt a growing dampness between her thighs. Inner muscles clenched and unclenched in anticipation.

'Is that what you want?'

'Oh, yes,' she confessed, a germ of fear that he would be too large for her no contest for her willingness to try. She licked her lips, hungry at the prospect, already sliding down his zip to slip her hand inside. She squeezed them gently through his silk underwear, so sheer the fabric hid nothing of him, before gliding the back of her nails up his length. 'Yes, please.'

He groaned and grabbed her wrist in a hand made of steel. 'Then you will have me,' he said, his voice thick around the edges, 'but not like this. When I come, I want to be inside you.'

He wasn't slow after that. He wasted no time lifting her from the circle of her fallen dress and spinning her onto the cloud-soft bed, laying her down almost reverentially upon the coverlet. His trousers lasted no longer than a second after that. His underwear but a blink.

She caught her breath. Before her stood a god, broad-shouldered and hard chested and sculpted from flesh that had been fired in the kiln of burning need. A flame still flickered in his dark eyes, while his thick erection swayed proudly before him. Hungry. Seeking.

Magnificent.

No mere boy like that other one whose name had suddenly vanished from her mind, but a man, fully—no—*perfectly* formed.

And she knew what he was seeking and her mouth went dry as he knelt with one knee on the bed and every drop of moisture in her body headed south.

He leaned over her, smoothing the tangle of her hair. 'Suddenly I'm not the one who's over-dressed,' he murmured and remedied that in-equality with a smooth sweep of his hands that bared her totally to him. She revelled at his swift intake of air, before his mouth fell upon hers, his tongue plundering her mouth while his hands plundered her body, seeking treasure, giving pleasure. Spreading heat.

Every touch, every kiss, every stroke of skin against skin building the heat, so that she thought she would self-combust.

'Alesander,' she gasped when his fingers circled that tightly wound bud that seemed right now to be the centre of her existence.

'I know,' he said, lifting his mouth from her nipple, simultaneously soothing her with his words, only to build on her distress with his clever fingers and heated mouth.

But he didn't know. He couldn't, or surely he would *do* something. 'Please!' she begged, breathless and burning up in a firestorm that threatened to overwhelm her.

And he left her for a moment, a moment where air rushed in against her heated skin and she could catch her breath. A moment before he was back, his body poised over hers.

'Tell me what you want,' he said, stroking her sex more purposefully now, the tips of his fingers venturing inside, teasing her, driving her inner muscles wild.

Oh God, she thought, as momentarily relief evaporated in another heated surge. 'I want you.'

He smiled. 'Then you shall have me.' He dipped his mouth to hers as their bodies touched in the most intimate of connections.

He was big. She had known that from her first touch. When his tip nudged her entrance and lingered there, she feared he was too big. She was determined he wouldn't be. She was determined...

'Open your eyes,' he ordered, withdrawing from the kiss, 'and look at me.'

She blinked her eyes open, confused. 'Relax,' he said, dipping his head to kiss her lightly on the mouth. 'Relax and breathe.'

'You're so big. I don't know if I can—'

'Of course you can,' he whispered on another light-as-air kiss to one hard nipple this time, as his fingers joined the gentle assault, working their magic again around that tiny bud of nerves.

She moaned at the sudden spike of pleasure

and felt the pressure shift and deepen and closed her eyes, rolling her head back on the pillow.

'No,' he commanded. 'Keep your eyes open.'

'I can't.' Her protest was little more than a breath, the fever inside her mounting, the feeling of fullness inside her building as he edged inside her another delicious fraction. She gasped.

'Open them! I want to see your eyes when you come.'

She fought the compulsion to close her eyes and go with the sensation and did as he commanded, panting hard, opening her eyes to his darkly intent gaze. His brow was slick with sweat, his features achingly tight, and the need she saw so clearly etched upon his straining face only magnified the pressure of what he was doing to her and how he felt inside her and she knew she was on the very cusp of losing herself.

'Alesander,' she gasped, her fingers curled into his muscled flesh before she tipped over the edge and with one final thrust he drove himself home.

Dios, she was tight! She exploded around him like fireworks, muscles contracting in the most intimate of massages, and it was all he could do to grit his teeth and hang on. He wasn't ready for this to be over just yet.

He waited for her to wind down, whispering kisses over slick skin that glowed like satin in the moonlight. 'Better now?' he asked, his lips gliding over the shell-like curves of her ear. 'Feeling more relaxed?'

She nodded. 'Mmm,' she murmured. 'Lovely.'

'Excellent,' he said, slowly pulling back, waiting at the brink before powering back in. Her eyes opened—wide.

'What are you doing?' she asked as he drew back again.

'Giving you more of what you want.'

'Oh,' she said, surprise and a little wonder turning to delight in her eyes. 'Oh!' she cried, as he plunged to the hilt inside her, groaning at the feel of her hot body, a tight sheath around him as he pumped. He would not last long like this. There was no way…

He heard her cry out, a wild sound of release, before his own was rent from him, the note raw and savage and wrenched from a place deep inside—some place he'd never known existed.

CHAPTER ELEVEN

'I BROUGHT YOU COFFEE.'

Simone blinked, still half asleep and only half understanding what she'd heard. Something about coffee? And sure enough, the scent of freshly brewed coffee seemed to flavour air that was otherwise heavily laden with sex. Hardly surprising given they'd spent more time making love last night than sleeping.

But really, coffee? The man was built like a god, made love as if he actually cared that his partner climaxed, *and* he made coffee for her instead of demanding a beer?

She snuggled back into her pillow. She really must be dreaming.

'How are you feeling?'

Her eyes snapped open. *How am I what?* He was freshly showered and wearing crisp, fresh clothes—another of those tops that skimmed the surface of his skin and made you want to peel it off, and trousers that accentuated the long lean contours of his legs—and he really was pouring her a cup of coffee. She sat up, snagging the bedding over her breasts, and pushed hair gone wild back from her face.

Outside, the windows the bay sparkled under a warm sun, a perfect autumn day. Inside her barometer wasn't anywhere near as controlled.

'I'm—' shattered '—okay,' she said, knowing she must look closer to the word she'd left unsaid. After the night they'd just spent, she couldn't imagine what kind of mess she looked.

'I thought you might be feeling tender. It was wrong of me to make love to you again this morning,' he said, as easily as he might have asked her if she wanted milk in her coffee. 'I should have given you some time.'

'I'm not…I wasn't…'

'A virgin? No, I know, but it's clear you haven't had much experience.'

'I have had sex before, you know. Several times. *A lot* of times, actually.' She'd even had the odd orgasm before, although admittedly she'd had to assist, so hadn't last night been a revelation? 'I told you I'd been in a relationship.'

He smiled at that. 'Oh yes. The boyfriend. I remember.' He sipped his coffee as he looked out over the view of the bay. 'Perhaps he wasn't as experienced.'

God, he wasn't as well endowed, more like it! She stared at her coffee rather than at him, so she wouldn't be forced to make any more comparisons, beyond the width of their shoulders, or the muscled firmness of their flesh, for instance. She shrugged and slanted her eyes up, feeling his eyes on her, knowing she was expected to say something. 'He wasn't put together quite the same as you, that's all.'

He smiled at her over his shoulder. 'They say size isn't important.'

Oh, they're so very wrong.

And then she made the mistake of looking at the clock and saw it was almost noon and didn't even have to feign surprise. Her cup rattled against the saucer as she sat up urgently, still clutching the bedclothes to her. 'I need to call the hospital and check on Felipe.'

'I already have. He is resting comfortably.' He tossed her a robe—his robe, she realised, and it was all she could do not to lift it to her face and breathe in his scent. 'I thought you'd want to visit so I said we'd be in to see him before lunch.'

She shrugged the robe around her shoulders, strangely touched, finding the armholes. 'You didn't have to do that.'

'You don't want to see your grandfather?'

'No, I mean you didn't have to call. I didn't expect you to.'

He shrugged, looking out of the window at the view. 'You were asleep. I thought you would want to know. Do you have a problem with that?'

'Aren't you worried I might think you were actually capable of being nice?'

She was half joking, but he didn't seem to take it that way. He blinked. Slowly. 'Whatever you think of me, I am not a beast. I am certainly capable of extending common courtesy where it is merited. Besides, don't you think it would look odd if I did not ask after my new grandfather-in-law?'

He turned and stared at her for a moment, one wholly unsettling moment under an intensely dark gaze, that had her putting a hand to her unruly hair and imagining he must be wondering what he'd done to be stuck with her.

Then he crossed to the bed, lifted her chin and kissed her briefly on the lips. A peck, nothing more.

'Besides,' he said, her chin still in his hand, his eyes still searching her face, 'you know better than to read too much into it.'

He left her then to get up, leaving her utterly bewildered and baffled, and yes, sore when she made a move to get out of bed. So it was all part of the act of being a dutiful husband to his granddaughter? Nothing more than common courtesy?

Still, he hadn't had to call. He didn't need to impress anyone now. The deal had been made and they were married. There was no getting out of it for her. He didn't have to be thoughtful. And yet he had been.

She padded barefoot to the bathroom and wondered anew about the man she had married. The man who was now not only her husband, but her husband in every sense of the word.

Their deal was temporary, their marriage fated to last a few months, no more. But after a night like last night, when Alesander had blown her world apart and then bothered to kiss it back together again, he seemed almost the perfect package. And at times, almost a man she might even think about choosing for her husband—in some parallel universe where they had met under different circumstances without the history of deal-making and blackmail that lay festering between them.

Damn, damn and damn!

What was he doing to her, that she could even think of wanting him for her husband? Was she so blinded by his lovemaking that she had forgotten that this was nothing more than a business arrangement? Was she so blindsided that she had forgotten the sheer terror of a missed period?

She should never forget that feeling, not if she wasn't to be taken in again by someone who didn't care for her—who had never loved her—who she never wanted to see again.

Still cursing, she slipped out of the voluminous robe and stepped into the shower, lifting her face up into the spray.

Why had Alesander insisted on having sex? Why had he had to complicate things when their arrangement had been fail-safe? She'd known sex would complicate things. Sex always did.

But the land hadn't been enough for him and sex was the price he'd exacted from her.

A price she'd agreed to.

And no matter how mind-blowing the sex and the redemptive power of a potent kiss, was it a price worth paying?

The hospital let Felipe go home the next day, but only, they said, because Alesander had arranged a nurse to be there around the clock for him. But, they warned, it would not be for ever.

Still, Felipe seemed positive after the wedding. At least for a few weeks.

Winter was closing in around the vineyard, the leaves falling from the vines when she found him sitting in his usual chair, looking out over the near barren vineyard, his eyes half shuttered. He seemed not to notice her presence, even after she'd spoken to him, and so she assumed he was asleep, when she picked up his coffee cup and a gnarled limb reached out, a bony set of fingers grabbed her wrist. *'Mi nieta!'*

She jumped, and then laughed at her reaction. *'Sí.* What is it, Abuelo?'

'I have something to tell you,' he whispered. 'Something I have been meaning to tell you.' He craned his head around. 'Is Alesander here?'

She shook her head. 'He's out in the vineyard somewhere. Do you want me to get him?'

'No. What I want to say is for you, and you alone. Sit down here next to me.'

She pulled over a chair. 'What is it?'

He sighed, his breath sounding like a wheeze. 'I want to tell you. There is not much time left to me. I must tell you...'

'No, Abuelo, you mustn't think that way.'

He patted her hand as if she was the one who needed compassion and understanding. 'Listen to me, there is nothing the doctors can do for me now, but I can still tell you this, that since you came here, since your marriage, I have never been happier. I have you to thank for making the sun shine in my life again.'

'Please, Abuelo, there is no need.'

'There is every need. Don't you see what you have done? You have given me hope. You have reunited two families who have barely spoken to each other for more than a century.'

She dipped her head. If he only knew, he would not be proud at all. But still she managed a smile and patted his hand. 'I am glad that you are happy, Abuelo.'

'More than happy. The rift between our families goes back many years. I never thought to see it end. But Alesander, he is a fine man. He is like the son I never had.'

He stopped on a sigh and his head nodded down, and she thought that he had finished then, already drifting back into his memories and his regrets, when he suddenly looked up, glassy eyes seeking hers. 'Do you know what happened?'

'Alesander told me. One of your ancestors— your grandfather, was it?—he ran off and married the bride meant for an Esquivel groom.'

The old man nodded. 'Ah, *sí*, he did.' He laughed then, a cackle of delight, before his face grew serious again. 'But did he tell you what happened afterwards?'

'Only that it has resulted in a century of simmering rivalry and a cause of resentment between the two families ever since.'

'And the rest? Did he tell you the rest?'

She reeled back through her memories of her conversation with Alesander. 'No, I don't seem to recall anything else.'

He nodded. 'Ah, he didn't tell you, then—

probably for the best. Anyway, it doesn't matter now.'

'What is it, Abuelo?' she asked, the skin at the back of her neck crawling. 'What doesn't matter now?'

'Only that when it was too late—when he discovered his bride was married to another, Xalbeder Esquivel vowed revenge and that the Esquivel family would drive the Otxoas from their land once and for all. That has always been their goal. That is why we have had to fight them ever since.'

Felipe peered at her, his watery eyes glistening, his crooked mouth smiling in a way she had never seen before. 'Don't you see what you have achieved by your marriage to Alesander? The curse is lifted. The Esquivels can never drive us from our land because the Otxoas will be ones with this estate for ever. I am so proud of you, *mi nieta*, so very proud.'

She let him pull her to him and hug her, feeling wiry arms around her, feeling bony shoulder blades stripped of flesh through his thick shirt, feeling the earth fall beneath her feet. If he only knew what she had done.

Oh God, what had she done?

By her own hand she had signed away the Otxoas' last links to this land. And she hadn't just let it happen—she had made it happen. 'Please don't be proud, Abuelo,' she pleaded, feeling sick. 'I don't deserve it.'

'Bah.' He waved her objections away with a sweep of one gnarled wrist. 'You have made an old man with no hope very happy. I am only sorry I did not trust Alesander at first. I thought he was only interested in the land. But he loves you, I can tell. And the way you look at him, with such love in your eyes…'

'Abuelo…' she chided with tears in her eyes, trying to gently cut him off. She could not bear to hear more, least of all to hear him talk of a love that had no place in her marriage. 'Please don't.'

But Felipe was equally determined to finish. 'Please, hear me out. There is not much time left to me now, and it is selfish of me to hope for anything beyond a death that lets me slip away quietly in my sleep and rejoin my Maria, that should be all I wish. Yet still I wish for more. I wish with all my heart that there might be news of a child before I go.'

'You're not going anywhere, Abuelo!' she cried, holding his knotted fingers in hers, knowing that his wishes were for nothing, knowing there could never be a child.

'You will tell me,' he insisted, 'if there is news. Promise me you will tell me and put a smile on an old man's face before he dies.'

'I will tell you,' she said as the tears streamed down her face, 'I promise.'

'Don't cry for me,' he said, misinterpreting her tears. 'I am not worth crying over. I did not mean to make you sad.'

'I'm sorry,' she told him, with one final brief, desperate hug, 'I am so very sorry.' And she fled from the cottage in tears.

What had she done?

She ran on and on through the vineyard, her

emotions in turmoil, oblivious to the magnificent view and uncaring of the vines snatching on her hair and tugging at her clothes, totally gutted at what she had done.

She'd lied to her grandfather. Yes, to make his last days happy, it was true, but what consolation was that when she'd lost him everything he'd ever held precious in the process? The last of his vines and she'd as good as given them away.

And she'd piled lie upon lie upon lie until he believed so much in this fiction she'd created, that he was building an entire future based on this perfect marriage.

This perfect lie.

And he'd told her he was proud of her and he'd thanked her for saving the family, for breaking a vow of revenge and a curse on them for generations.

When she was the curse.

She'd betrayed Felipe and his trust in her. Betrayed his love for his only remaining relative, the only person he could put his faith and hope for the future in.

Lied to him and betrayed him by giving away all that he had left and held precious.

But seeping up through all the welter of emotions, through the tangle of her despair and her self-recrimination, there was a slow, simmering anger bubbling away inside the guilt and remorse.

For she too had been betrayed.

Because Alesander must have known!

All along, Alesander would have known about the vow to drive the Otxoas from their land. She might as well have offered it to him on a silver platter.

And then the land hadn't been enough and he'd wanted her too.

Was that part of the revenge? Was he laughing at her the whole time?

She felt sick. He'd played her for a fool.

She'd even imagined he cared.

Oh God.

She came to the edge of the property and the new fence where once she'd come in despair when she'd learned that Felipe was dying, and where she'd come up with a plan to make his last days happy.

A stupid plan.

A stupid woman to ever think it could ever work. A stupid woman to think she could pile lie upon lie and get off scot-free, with no consequences and no price to pay.

And she'd imagined that sex with Alesander was the price she'd had to pay.

No.

Knowing she'd betrayed the love and trust of the only family member she had left, the family member who was relying on her to save the family name from obliteration—this was the price she had to pay.

With a cry of anguish, she sagged, tear-streaked and heaving for air, against a trellis upright, ancient and thick. She clung to it, panting, looking out over the view that had once seemed so magical to her—the spectacular shoreline that curled jaggedly around in both directions, framing a brilliant blue sea, with the red-roofed town of Getaria nestled in behind the rocky headland—and she would swap it in a heartbeat to be back in a cramped student flat with noisy neighbours and lousy weather.

The whole time he would have known. The whole time he would have been laughing at her behind her back, thinking that she had achieved singlehandedly what his family had been unable to achieve in generations.

They would all laugh when she was gone. They were probably all laughing at her now, all in on the joke, just waiting for the old man to die.

And she'd gone to Alesander for help.

How could she ever face Felipe again?

'Simone!'

Oh God, she thought as his voice rang out again, closer this time. Not him. Anyone but him. She tried to disappear into the tangle of vines but in a blue and yellow sundress she was too easy to spot.

'Simone!' he said. 'At last.'

She turned her back to him, swiping at her tear-streaked face with her hands.

'Simone, Felipe said he'd upset you.'

'Go away,' she said without turning around.

'What's wrong?'

'Just leave me alone.'

He took no notice. He came up behind her and put a hand to her shoulder. A touch she'd become so used to. A touch that had warmed her in places she daren't confess. A touch that now left her cold. 'Simone, what's going on?'

'Don't touch me!' she cried, spinning around and shoving away his hand. 'Don't you ever touch me again!'

'What the hell is going on? What's happened to make you this way?'

'What do you think is wrong? Why didn't you tell me the whole story?'

'What story?'

'Your potted history of the troubles between the Esquivels and the Otxoas.'

He frowned. 'What about it? What am I supposed to have missed?'

'The bit you so conveniently left out. The bit about the Esquivels vowing to drive the Otxoas from their land!'

He shrugged his shoulders, his hands palm up in the air. 'What about it? I didn't think it was important.'

'*What about it?* Are you kidding me? Do you think I would have ever married you if I had known that your agenda the entire time was to run Felipe—to run us—off our land?'

'*Dios!* This marriage was all your idea. Don't you forget that. You were the one who came up with it. You were the one who so desperately needed it!'

'And you were the one who insisted on the land being part of the deal! Because you knew, didn't you? You knew all along that your family wanted us off. And because you saw a way of getting rid of my family from this land for ever!'

'Listen to yourself! Do you really think I care about something that happened more than a hundred years ago? Do you honestly believe I set out with the intention of banishing the Otxoas from their land?'

'What am I supposed to think, when the land is the one thing you expressly demanded? And now my grandfather thinks I've saved this family from some kind of curse and all I know is that I've made it happen. I've brought it down upon us. How do you think I feel about that? How do you think I feel?'

She broke down, her knees collapsing beneath her, sending her limp and sagging into the ground.

His hands caught her at her shoulders, pulling her up, pulling her towards him. 'What do you care about the land anyway? You're going home. You said yourself you don't belong here.'

She pushed with all her might against him. 'And that makes it okay? That's your defence?' She lashed at him with her fists, pounding at his unyielding chest, but he did not let her go and so she punched harder. 'Don't touch me!'

He held her at arm's length and still she managed to lash out at him. He grabbed her wrists, locking them within the iron circle of his own and pulled her in close. 'What the hell is wrong with you?'

'You knew,' she said, angling her face and her

accusations higher. 'You knew all the time about the land and the curse. That land means everything to him and now you've taken it.'

His dark eyes gleamed dangerously down at her, his hot breath fanning her face, the cords on his neck standing out in rigid lines. 'And you made a deal, remember! You were the one who turned up on my doorstep begging.'

Fruitlessly she wrenched against the prison of his hands. 'But you knew! All the time you knew!'

'So what? The damned curse means nothing to me!'

'But it does to him!' She was so rigid she felt she might snap. She glared up at him. 'It does to him and I hate you for what you've done!'

He growled and shook his head slowly from side to side, his dark eyes like magnets, their pull insistent and strong. 'Oh no, you don't. You don't hate me at all.'

His slow words and his rich accent stroked her like a slow velvet hand, and she felt the first unmistakable frisson of fear.

And the first unmistakable frisson of excitement.

No! That would be to let him win. She tugged desperately at her wrists. 'Let me go.'

He tugged her back so she ended up even closer to the hard wall of his chest, his mouth turned up at the corners, his eyes never deviating from hers, and she knew what he intended and there was no way…

'Let me go!'

He stepped closer. She stepped back. He took another step and this time her step was more of a stumble, until she found the old support she'd been clinging to before against her back. She'd welcomed it for its solidity then. Now she cursed it for preventing her escape, leaving her sandwiched between it and him.

He let her hands go then, to frame her face in his hands, his fingers deep in her hair, and she reached back, clinging to the support, keeping her hungry fingers away from him.

'What are you doing?' she asked, her heart

beating too fast, too frantically, already knowing the answer.

So that when his mouth crashed down on hers it came as no surprise. His vehemence did. There was no remaining unaffected—his hot mouth and tongue seemed to want to plunder her very soul.

What had he done to her? she wondered as his tongue licked like a trail of flames across her throat. What had he reduced her to?

Feelings, the answer came back, as she gave herself up into his kiss and gave him back all he was offering her.

Feelings.

He had awoken her to feeling and she was a slave to it. *Slave to him.*

Her hands abandoned the support behind her. She was pulling at his clothes as fast as he was pulling at hers. The zip of her dress was undone, the tail of his shirt was tugged free. Her breasts exposed to his mouth, his chest was bared to her seeking fingers.

And his hands were at the hem of her dress,

sliding the fabric up her legs, sliding down again once he'd hooked his fingers into her underwear and swept them away.

Air brushed the sensitive folds of her flesh. Cool air against hot torrid flesh.

'Alesander,' she cried, half plea, half protest as she battled to release him, a battle made harder because he was so hard.

'I know,' he muttered against her throat, her jaw, her mouth as he helped her. 'I know.'

And then he lifted her and he was right there, at her entrance, and she thought her world could end and she wouldn't care so long as he was inside her first.

She cried out when he pulled her down onto him. She cried out when he pulled back, knowing she'd been wrong. Because she didn't ever want her world to end. Not when her world made it possible to feel like this.

He pounded into her, angry and insistent, and angrily, insistently she clenched her muscles and hung onto him, only to welcome him back, her need building with each desperate thrust.

'Do you hate me now?' he asked, thrusting again, his voice barely a grunt. 'Do you still hate me?'

Her body was alive with sensation, her senses dancing wildly along a dangerous line that any moment they might teeter off into an abyss, and there was no way she could not answer honestly.

'I hate you,' she said, *but not because of Felipe or the land or a vow of revenge that was made more than a century ago, but because of what you do to me.* 'I will always hate you.'

He answered with a thrust that threw her head crashing back against the beam. He followed it with another and then another, each one deeper than the first. Each one more desperate, more insistent. Each one building on that screaming tension building inexorably inside her.

He won't make me come, she told herself, knowing the assault he was capable of, clamping down on that eventuality with all her muscles and all her might. Knowing what was in store if she just let him. *I won't let him. I won't give him the satisfaction.*

And so she fought and resisted and battled against the torrent of sensations he subjected her to and tried to imagine herself back in her tiny flat in Melbourne, where this man and these feelings would be just a distant memory.

But it was too hard a task, too much to ask, with his mouth at her throat and on her lips, his hands hot on her breasts and fingers tight against her nipples and his hard cock thrusting deep inside her. It was all…impossible.

And like a cough suppressed because you were in polite company, but that refused to be suppressed, so that when it was unleashed it was ten times greater than the original would have ever been, her release came upon her with the relentless force of a tornado, picking her up and spinning her effortlessly into its whirling spout, drawing her higher, ever higher in its never ending spiral until she came in a flash of colour and heated sensation and felt herself spat out of the tornado's spout. She drifted down to the earth, or maybe that was just her legs as he let them down, her fight gone as she rested limply under the weight of his body against hers.

And she hated that he could do this to her—turn argument into a storm, turn anger into passion.

She hated him because he could reduce her to a whimpering mess of nerve endings.

She hated him because she loved him.

Oh God, where had that come from?

She tried to wish the unwanted thought away. She tried to deny it. But the truth of it refused to be wished away or denied. It floated like a balloon let loose, flying high, freed of the shackles that could pull it down.

She loved him.

The concept was so foreign. So unexpected. And yet it explained so much of why she wanted to be with him and why at the same time she feared it so.

She loved him because of what he could do to her and how he made her feel.

She loved him and she hated him because at any moment he would look at her smugly and declare himself the victor of this particular encounter.

Except not this time, it seemed. *'Mierda!'* he cursed, and pulled himself free, pulling himself away as if she was poison. 'You're not on the Pill.'

She blinked, still in recovery mode, not sure why it was an issue. 'You know I'm not.'

'I didn't use protection.'

CHAPTER TWELVE

'OH MY GOD!' She was still reeling from her discovery. The last thing she needed was *that*. She put a hand to her head, recovery mode short-circuited by a panic that unfurled with a vengeance as she remembered another time, another fear that things had come unstuck, even after protection had been used.

But this time there had been no protection. No defence.

Oh God, was she destined to live her life making love to the wrong men, narrowly escaping disaster with one, only to hurtle headlong into catastrophe with the next?

She'd known from the very beginning that having sex with Alesander was a bad idea. Why had he not realised the complications that could result? Had he not realised how serious they could be?

Her panicked brain morphed to anger. 'How could you do that?' she cried. 'How could you be so stupid?'

Her answer was the thwack of the flat of his hand high above her head against the beam supporting her. 'Did you ask me to put on a condom?'

'And so it's my fault—?' even though she hadn't given protection a thought, and she knew she hadn't, but damned if she was going to accept the blame '—because you can't control yourself?'

'And you didn't want it?'

'Did I ask for it? Did I ever ask for sex from you, or did you simply demand it, as you always did?'

'You enjoyed it. You know you did.'

'That's not the same thing and you know it.'

He turned away from her then, his shoulders heaving, and she sensed the loss of him even as she celebrated the relief that came from the distance between them, and she wondered at the tangle of those conflicting emotions and wondered if love made sense of it all.

Ever since that first day in his apartment it had been the same, the relentless push and pull confusing her thoughts and tangling her intentions.

But now there was something else to confuse her thoughts and add to the tangle in her mind.

What if she were pregnant?

She'd lived this nightmare once before—the overwhelming fear of being pregnant to a man who didn't want her—the fear, the terror of thinking that she was, the utter helplessness at not knowing.

But beyond that, the endless soul-searching at being tempted to do something she knew she could never do. She wasn't a religious woman, her parents had brought her up with no particular belief systems that told her she should act one way or another and she had grown up believing she could do anything she wanted in the world. But, when push came to shove, she had learned that there were some places she could not go, some lines she could not cross.

What were the chances?

Luck had been with her that time, sending her a belated period that had been accompanied by a torrent of tears—grateful tears. As it was, she had held herself together these last few months by a tenuous thread. She could not have coped if she'd been pregnant with Damon's child.

And now the nightmare was happening all over again. Again the fear. Again the hoping. Again the anxious, endless wait and the anguished sleepless nights until she knew, one way or the other.

She couldn't be pregnant. She was leaving when this was over. She had to leave. She had to get away before he discovered the truth.

Because falling in love with Alesander had never been part of the deal.

'It was wrong of me,' he admitted suddenly, completely blindsiding her. 'I should never have made love to you. Not here. Not like this.'

She channelled shock into rational thought and turned her panicked mind to calculating dates, needing to be able to hope. 'It might be okay,' she said, needing to believe it. 'It's early in my cycle. It would be unlucky.' But then she'd been lucky last time. Did this kind of luck get balanced out? Was it her turn to be unlucky?

He had his back to her, refusing to look at her.

Two facts that didn't escape her. 'Luck does not come into it. It shouldn't have happened!'

She swiped up her knickers from the ground with as much dignity as she could muster, balling them in her fist, not bothering to further humiliate herself by stopping to tug them on now. 'You're so right,' she said. 'Maybe you might try remembering that next time.'

Alesander swung around. There wouldn't be a next time. Damn her, there shouldn't have been a *this time*!

He was a man of needs, it was true. He always had been. But never since his first wild encounter with a woman, when he'd barely been a teenager and she was a wanton who'd let his night time fantasies play out in her hot hands and hot mouth and who'd given him a gold-plated initiation to the pleasures of the flesh, had he been so unprepared and made such a mistake. He'd used up all the luck he was planning on ever needing that time.

Because he wasn't a teenager any more.

There were no excuses.

Except to blame her.

That was the one thing he could do.

Because she did this to him. She was the one who reduced him to his basest level and his basest needs. She was the one who drove him crazy and made him blind with lust when he needed to be thinking straight.

'There can be no child!'

'My God, do you actually think I want one?'

'Why not? When you're the one who stands to gain the most by prolonging this relationship.'

'You think? Why the hell would I want to prolong spending time with you? No, I'm going home when this is over. A child of yours is hardly the kind of souvenir I want or need to take with me.'

'And if it's already happened? You can't just wish it away.'

'Damn you, Alesander. And whose fault would it be if there was? I *told* you I didn't want to have sex with you. I told you it was the only way to guarantee there could be no complications. But did you listen to me? No. Because Mr Can't-Live-Without-Sex couldn't exercise a bit of self-control.'

'And you haven't enjoyed it? You didn't cry out in pleasure every time you came? Every time I took you there?'

'And that's relevant, because? You know damned well that I didn't want to have sex with you. You were the one who changed the terms.'

'Terms you agreed to!'

'Only because you threatened to tell Felipe our marriage was a sham if I didn't!'

How else was he supposed to get her to agree? 'You wanted it. You wanted me from that first time in my apartment. Do you think I couldn't smell your need? Do you think I didn't know then and there that you were gagging for it?'

The crack of her palm against his cheek punctuated the argument. For a long moment he said nothing, his nostrils flaring, his eyes like dark— *angry*—pits. 'You never were very good at dealing with the truth.'

She squeezed her eyes shut. Oh God, the truth. What was the truth any more? She'd told so many lies she was beginning to forget where truth ended and the lies began. She'd lied to Felipe every time she saw him and pretended to be happy in her marriage. She'd lied to herself pretending that she didn't want Alesander and then burning up with him at night. And now she was slapping a man she'd only just finished convincing herself that she loved. But there was one indisputable truth that he could not argue with. 'If we are talking truths, then I know of one truth you cannot deny—that if we had kept to the original terms of the contract, if we had never had sex, then we wouldn't be having this conversation now, because the chances of conceiving a baby would never have been an issue.'

Silence reigned between them, letting in the sounds of the vineyard, the rustle of leaves in the breeze and the cry of seabirds amid the heavy weighted silence of blame and regret.

'So when will you know?'

She shook her head, dragging in air. 'Three weeks? Most likely less.' *Hopefully less.* She swallowed, a sick feeling roiling in her gut. Would he ask her to make sure? He was a man of the world. He would know there were options. At least there were in Australia...

'I won't...' she started. 'I can't...'

'That is not our way!' he simply said, putting a full stop on that particular conversation. 'Three weeks, you say?'

'It's early in my cycle, which is good...well... it's better. Safer.'

'*Sí.*' He frowned. 'I can wait that long. And meanwhile I will show you that you are wrong, that I can exercise control and live without sex.'

She laughed, the sound bitter. 'Don't you think it's a little late for that?'

Maybe it was, but he could do with the time away from her. He'd enjoyed her in his bed these past few weeks, and perhaps he'd enjoyed her too much. Perhaps that was the problem.

Putting distance between them, putting up barriers, might be the best thing for them. Felipe was growing weaker—the march of his disease relentless, the damage wrought becoming more apparent by the day. Soon she'd be going home and there was no point getting used to having her around.

And he didn't want her getting used to being around. His women were supposed to be temporary. That was the way he liked it.

That was the way he'd always liked it.

They were almost back at the cottage when they heard it, a crash followed by a muffled cry.

'Felipe!' she screamed alongside him, suddenly bolting for the door.

'They won't let him come home,' she sniffed, sitting in a hospital waiting room chair, repeating the words the doctor had just delivered. 'I should have been there. I should never have left him.'

'It wouldn't have made any difference. Felipe

is ill. His bones are weak. If it didn't happen today, it could have been tomorrow or the next day.'

'But I should have been there.'

He pulled her closer, his arm around her shoulders. 'It's not your fault.'

'Felipe hates hospitals. It will kill him being away from his vines.'

'Simone, he's dying. He's too sick now to be at home. You can't look after him. You can't watch him twenty-four hours a day.'

And she sniffed again and knew that there was nothing he could say or do that would make her feel better. Felipe had needed her and she hadn't been there.

And where she had been and what she'd been doing—oh God—was Felipe to get his wish for a baby after all? Was that to be yet another price she would pay for her lies?

She buried her face in her hands and cried, 'I should have been there.'

Felipe's condition steadily deteriorated after that, the break in his hip ensuring he would stay bedridden. Simone spent as much time with him as possible. He had moments of great lucidity, where he would talk about Maria and how they had met and the fiestas where he had courted her.

He had moments of rambling confusion, where he would tumble words in Spanish and Basque and English all together and make no sense at all.

At night Alesander would collect her from the hospital and take her back to the apartment and make sure she ate something before she fell into bed and woke up to do it all over again.

He watched her withdraw into herself, watched the shadows grow under her eyes, watched the haunted look on her features and he marvelled at her strength.

And he ached for her.

God, how he ached for her.

He wanted her so much. He wanted to hold her and hug her and soothe away her pain. He wanted to make love to her and put life and light back into her beautiful blue eyes.

But, true to his word, he did not make a move on her.

He doubted she even noticed, and that made him feel no better.

At night he watched her sleeping, watching the steady rise and fall of her chest, her beautiful face at peace for a few short hours until she woke and the pain of grief and imminent loss returned.

'You don't have to go in every day,' he'd said to her after the first week. 'Have a day to yourself. Relax.'

But she'd shaken her head. 'I have to go,' she'd said. 'I'm all he has. He's all I have.'

And he'd ached for her that she had lost so much in her short life.

And what she hadn't lost, he'd taken.

They'd made a deal, he told himself, a contract, and that made him feel no better at all.

'He's all I have,' she'd said.

And it twisted in his gut that he didn't figure in her deliberations at all. Was there no place for him? Did he mean nothing to her after the months they'd spent together? After the nights when she'd lain so slick with sweat and satisfied in his arms?

Sure, they'd always planned to part and go their separate ways when Felipe died and their contract came to an end. But why should knowing that he meant so little sit so uncomfortably with him?

An ambulance brought Felipe home to die, the two nurses setting up his bed near the window of the cottage where he'd been born so he could look out over the vineyard where he'd lived his entire life. A day, they warned her, she'd have with him. Maybe two at the most.

She spent the first day sitting by his side, talking to him when he was awake enough to listen, about what was going on in the vineyard or about what life was like in Australia. Every now and then she was certain he had taken his last breath, and she would hold her own as he would grow absolutely still, only for the next breath to shudder from the depths of his sunken chest and make her jump. Sometimes his breathing came so fast he could have been running a race. And other times he fidgeted and shifted restlessly, muttering words she couldn't understand.

On the second day she grew more used to the breathing. Or maybe she just grew used to not knowing which might be his final breath. Still she expected his death to come that day.

On the third day she sat alongside the bed, feeling exhausted. He was eating nothing, drinking less, and still he held on. It was killing her watching him—listening to his stop–start breathing and hearing the bubbling gurgle in his chest. She held his hand, talking to him when it seemed he might be awake, sponging his brow when he seemed upset or agitated.

The fidgeting grew worse. Felipe fidgeted with the blanket again, murmuring words she couldn't understand. She touched her hand to his to calm him and chided him gently, 'You're cold, Abuelo. You should put your hands under the blanket.'

One of the nurses took her aside when he had

calmed into a sleep and she had risen to stretch her legs. 'It's a sign,' the nurse said. 'His circulation is slowing. His whole body is closing down.'

'But why is it taking so long?' she cried. She didn't want her grandfather to die, but neither did she want to see him suffer. 'And he's so restless at times. He wanted to go quietly in his sleep. Why does he fidget so much?'

The nurse smiled and took her hands. 'Sometimes the living can't let them go. And other times people can't let themselves go. Sometimes there are loose ends or plans left unfinished. Is there anything you know of that he is worried about? Are there loose ends he wanted tied up?'

Simone shook her head. 'I thought he wanted to be reunited with Maria.'

'And there's nothing else he might feel has been left undone?'

She closed her eyes and sighed. Because there was one thing Felipe had wished for.

But there was no chance of that now. Her period had come the week before. The much anticipated period that would tell her if her passionate encounter with Alesander amidst the vines had resulted in a child.

It had not.

She hadn't bothered to tell Alesander and he hadn't bothered to ask, whether because he'd lost count of the days or merely lost interest she didn't know. Maybe because he'd believed her when she'd assured him it would be okay. Maybe because all he'd ever cared about was the land and any day now it would be his—every day brought him closer to his goal.

Whatever, Alesander had stopped caring. He didn't want to know.

And then, when it all came down to it, Felipe didn't need to know either.

She looked over at him, shrunken and tormented on the bed, biting her lip. Would it matter to tell one more tiny lie? One more on top of all the others?

No, she decided, watching his busy fingers worry the bedding again.

One more tiny lie would make no difference at all now.

She sat down beside him, took his cold fingers in her own and squeezed them gently. 'Abuelo, it's Simone.'

One of the nurses called him, warning him it was close, and for a while he wondered whether he should even be there. He'd kept his distance the last few days she'd been living at the cottage again. Felipe was her grandfather and after the month they'd had, he wondered if she even wanted him there.

But he couldn't stay away.

She would be leaving soon. Once Felipe died, there would be no reason for her to stay. She would pack her things and return to her home and her studies in Melbourne.

He would probably never see her again.

He needed to see her again before that happened.

Besides, she was about to lose the only person she cared about in the world. She needed someone to be there for her.

He wanted that person to be him.

He wanted her to know he was there for her, even if she didn't care.

He stepped into the tiny cottage, his eyes taking a few seconds to adjust to the gloom after being outside, and saw Simone sit down next to the bed where her wizened grandfather lay.

'Abuelo, it's Simone.' She took his cold fingers in hers, wishing him her warmth.

He muttered something low and hard to understand, but he was awake and still listening.

'Abuelo, I have some good news.' Tears squeezed from her eyes at the lie she was about to tell. One more lie to follow all the others, but maybe this would be the end of it, she told herself. And if it let him go, maybe this lie was the most important of all of them. 'You got your wish, Abuelo. I…I am expecting a baby. And I am hoping with all my heart it will be a boy because then we will call him after you. We will name him Felipe.'

'Ah,' the old man said on a gasp, his hand jerking, tugging her closer as his jaw worked up and down. 'Ah!'

She leaned over him. 'What is it?' she asked.

'Happy,' he gasped. *'Gracias, mi nieta, gracias.'*

The effort almost seemed too much as he sagged back into the pillows, and she thought he was finished until she heard his thready voice. 'Maria...Maria is here. I must go to her.'

'Sí,' she said, nodding as tears filled her eyes and spilled onto the bedding. 'She has been waiting for you. She will be so happy to see you again.'

How long it was after that she couldn't tell. She only knew that one of the nurses finally touched her on the shoulder. 'He's gone,' she said, and Simone nodded, because she had sensed the exact moment Felipe had gone to join his wife.

It was done.

CHAPTER THIRTEEN

SHE WAS PREGNANT.

Alesander reeled from the room, needing air, blindsided by Simone's confession to a dying man. She was pregnant and she hadn't even bothered to tell him—*the child's father*—first.

He should be angry.

How long had she known? A few days? A week?

No, not just angry. He should be furious.

This was exactly what he had feared all along, and it was really happening. Their temporary arrangement had suddenly got a whole lot more complicated.

And she hadn't even bothered to tell him.

He turned his face to the sky, into air now as crisp and cool as the Txakolina wine produced from the grapes in these vineyards, searching for answers.

So why wasn't he furious?

Instead he felt almost…relieved.

He breathed out a breath he hadn't realised he'd been holding.

Because she couldn't go home now.

Strange how that idea suddenly seemed so right. He would not let her go. She was bearing their child.

She would have to stay now.

Felipe was dead.

Strange, how it still took so long to sink in, even when you knew it was true.

Desolate, exhausted, she gently placed her grandfather's hand over his chest and rose from her chair, kissing his snowy whiskered cheeks one final time. 'Goodbye, Abuelo,' she said. 'Sleep tight.'

Numb and bone-weary, she left the bedside chair that had been her home for the last three days. Her back ached, her head hurt and there was a hole where her heart had once been.

Abuelo was dead.

There was nothing for her here now.

Soon she would pack her things and return home. But not even that thought brought her comfort.

'Simone?'

She looked up to see Alesander standing in the doorway and he looked so familiar and strong that for a moment her heart kicked over, as if there was life left in it after all. And then she remembered that he was supposed to mean nothing to her and it died again.

'He's gone,' she said, finally accepting it, and with acceptance came a torrent of tears.

She would have fallen if he hadn't been there to catch her. 'I know,' he said, wrapping his arms around her and pulling her against his chest and he felt both a friend and a stranger. How long since he had held her in his arms like this?

And he felt so good, so solid and warm. He smelled so good. She drank in his scent in greedy heaving gasps, relishing the masculine scent of him while she could, knowing she would miss it when she was gone. He stroked her back until the crying jag finished. 'Come on. I'll take you home.'

Home.

Where was that?

Once upon a time she had been desperate to leave Spain and get back to Melbourne.

But now?

Now she'd fallen in love with a craggy coast-line and cerulean sea and with vines that tangled above her head and gave the grapes a view of the sea.

Now she'd fallen in love with a man she had to say goodbye to.

Now she wasn't sure where home really was.

He led her to the car, drove her back to the apartment as day turned to night. He didn't talk while the lift carried them upstairs, he just stood with his arm around her shoulders and never before had she appreciated anyone's silence or support more.

She let him lead her through the darkened apartment to the bedroom with its big wide bed and strip her down to her underwear. There was nothing sexual about the way he touched her. It was like a parent undressing a child before putting them to bed. Gentle. Caring. But with purpose.

She clambered in, almost crying out in pleasure at the bed's welcoming embrace. She'd imagined he'd leave her then to sleep, but a moment later he surprised her by joining her, pulling her into his arms and just holding her close to him. She wasn't worried, he hadn't touched her for the best part of a month.

She felt him press his lips to her head.

She felt...*safe*.

Empty and numb, but safe in this man's embrace. And right now, that meant more than anything.

'Thank you,' she whispered against his chest, the wiry hairs of his chest tickling her lips.

'What for?' he said, his mouth in her hair.

'For just being here.'

He lifted her chin with one hand. In the darkened room she sensed rather than saw his eyes on her, she felt the fan of his breath on her cheek, before he dipped his head and pressed his lips to hers.

No more than a touch of flesh against flesh, and then another, just as brief, but she sighed at the contact, sighing at the memories it stirred inside her, whispers of past kisses like the tendrils on the vines, catching and tugging at her senses.

Oh, how she'd missed his mouth.

How she would miss it when she was gone.

How she would miss him.

She blinked into the darkness, and the darkness didn't matter because it was as if she could see. Suddenly she was aware of the press of her body against his, aware of every place their bodies touched, aware of the stroke of his long-fingered hand over her skin.

Suddenly she was aware of the tension in his body, as if he was holding himself rigid to protect her, so that he could comfort her.

And numbness turned to life as comfort turned to need.

Tomorrow she would have to make plans. There was a funeral to be arranged. There would have to be papers signed and transferred.

She would have to make arrangements to return home.

But that was tomorrow.

First, there was tonight.

Maybe their last night?

'Alesander?' she whispered, her toes brushing his shin, her breasts tight and aching in her bra and a pooling heat growing in her belly.

'Yes?'

She tilted her head higher, found his lips with hers and whispered over them the words, 'Kiss me again.'

He made a sound, strangled and thick in the back of his throat, even as he pulled her closer to him. 'If I do—'

'I know,' she said, smoothing her hand down the long gentle slide of his back, to the small of his back and the curve of his behind, memorizing him through her skin. 'I need it. I need to feel alive.'

She didn't have to ask him twice. His mouth took hers, warm and real and alive, and she drank in his taste and his heat, as welcoming as the mattress beneath her, while his hands tangled in her hair or swept down the length of her, his touch so sweet—so missed—it made her cry into his mouth.

Then he lifted his head. 'Are you sure it's all right?' he asked, and she thought how sweet he was to ask, as if finally she mattered, not just the sex.

'It's perfect.'

He did not rush. It was not like that heated encounter in the vineyard. He took his time reacquainting himself with her body, noticing the places where her flesh dipped lower or her hip bones jutted higher. She'd lost weight while she'd looked after Felipe, he could tell. He would see that she ate from now on. She would have to eat.

He slipped off her bra and her sigh sounded like thanks. He cupped her perfect breast in his hand and she whimpered with need.

'You're beautiful,' he told her as he lifted himself over her, not knowing how he could have let her alone for so long; promising himself he never would again, knowing he would never have to.

She opened herself to him and his fingers found her slick and wet for him. She cried out as his thumb teased her sensitive nub, arching on the bed. He should linger there, he knew. He should take his time and pleasure her properly and he would.

Next time.

This time he knew what she wanted.

He didn't reach for a condom. He didn't need one. She was pregnant already, with his child in her belly.

He stroked the flat of his hand over her mound, over that belly, over one perfect breast that would feed his child, while he steadied his swaying erection with the other, finding her centre, finding her hot and slick and oh, so sweet.

And, oh God, he thought as he entered her in one long thrust, and she angled her hips to meet him, so welcoming.

He kissed her then, in that exquisite moment of joining, making love to her mouth while buried to the hilt inside her.

It was mind-shattering.

And then he moved and it got better.

He groaned. He would not last. It had been a long time. Too long. And her needy cries and hungry fingers on his skin told him she needed this as much as he did.

Maybe more.

She moved both with him and against him, tight and hot around him, and so perfect he wanted to control it and stay this way for ever.

His traitorous body wouldn't let him, the slip and slide of flesh against flesh compelling and urgent and unable to be withstood.

And when she came apart around him, any last shred of control was blown away in the fallout.

With a cry he unleashed himself inside her, pumping into her perfect body as her muscles tightened around him and urged him on.

Spent, he rolled off her, tucking her close against him as ragged breathing eased and their bodies calmed. He kissed her hair and she nestled into him.

'Thank you,' she whispered and he kissed her on the head again. He lay like that in the dark, listening as her breathing steadied and feeling her body relax as she slipped inexorably towards sleep.

How had they come to this place, he wondered, where he was so comfortable with her staying— where he was comfortable with the concept of her having his child?

Where he was happy with it?

When had the change occurred?

And why?

He had no answers as the woman beside him slumbered in his arms. Maybe tomorrow, with the cool clear light of a new day, it would make more sense.

Already he looked forward to the morning, but for more reasons than that alone. Because come the new day the woman beside him would awaken and they would have sex again. Come the new day she might be feeling better and more in the mood for talking.

Surely then she would remember to tell him about the baby.

CHAPTER FOURTEEN

SHE WOKE IN his arms feeling sad, but better than she had in weeks. Warm, cossetted and maybe even a little loved. For it would be nice to think Alesander loved her, just a little, after she was gone. Because last night had proved one thing to her, and that was that she loved him.

He'd helped her feel alive when all she'd felt was numb. He'd shown her that after death, life went on. He'd given her a gift of life-affirming sex gift-wrapped in his tenderness, and she loved him all the more for it.

Leaving him would kill her, but she would have the memory of their lovemaking to keep her warm at night.

She woke wanting to make love again, knowing there would not be many more times, but he gently put her away, kissing her on the forehead and telling her that he didn't want her to overdo it, and he would make breakfast for her. Confused and a little hurt, she wondered if already he was withdrawing, in preparation for her leaving.

Then, all during breakfast—while she sat and ate the omelette he'd insisted on making for her—he seemed to be watching her, almost as if he were waiting for something. Was it that she was leaving or did he worry she might suddenly collapse in a heap again? Was that the reason for his sudden care?

'Is something wrong?' she asked, putting down her knife and fork when she caught him looking sideways at her again.

'I don't know,' he said disingenuously. 'I just wondered if there's something you wanted to tell me.'

She blinked. 'Like what?'

'Oh, who can say?' he said, the corners of his mouth turning up. 'Can you think of anything you might be keeping from me that maybe you should share? That I might be interested in hearing? A secret, perhaps?'

A chill descended her spine.

Surely he couldn't know.

Not that. There was no way he could know that.

They'd barely spoken in the last month and she hadn't said anything last night in the depths of passion. *Had she?* 'I don't have any secrets.'

'None? Nothing at all to tell me?'

Nothing that you would want to hear.

'I can understand you might be nervous about telling me,' he said, and all the while she was thinking, *He knows.* 'I know I've warned you enough times, but I'd like to think our relationship has changed. I don't want you to think there is anything you can't share with me.'

She swallowed, both nervous and excited in case it meant he felt the same way. Could it be possible? Had Alesander fallen in love with her too? The way he had treated her last night made her want to believe it. And the way he was looking at her now made her think it might even be possible.

He took her hand in his and squeezed it gently.

'You don't have to be nervous,' he prompted. 'You can tell me.'

'Well,' she said, her heart hammering in her chest, trying to find the courage to tell him the truth. 'Maybe there is one thing.'

He smiled encouragingly. 'I thought so. What is it?'

His fingers were warm and reassuring around her hand, his eyes dark with promise and so she relaxed and smiled. 'Then I guess it's time you knew. Alesander, I love you.'

A blank stare met her confession. 'What?'

He shook his head. 'Isn't there something else? I thought you were going to tell me about the baby. When were you going to tell me about the baby?'

'The baby? There is no baby.'

He dropped her hand. 'But I heard you tell Felipe...'

Oh God. And she had just told him that she loved him. 'You were there?'

'Of course I was there. The nurses called me—told me it was close. And I heard you. You told

Felipe you were pregnant, that we were having a child. You told him you were going to call it Felipe. I heard you!'

'Alesander...' she swallowed '...you have to understand—'

He spun out of his chair, strode away across the room, raking the fingers of one hand through his hair, his other on his hip. 'Damn it, you said it. Why the hell would you do that if it wasn't true?'

'Because it's what Felipe wanted to hear. It's what he needed to hear!'

'Felipe could barely hear you let alone understand that!'

'No, listen to me, that day in the vineyard, the day he fell—he told me that day that it was his greatest wish that there be news of a child before he died. He wanted to know his family would go on after he died.'

'But that was the day—'

'I know.'

'We had unprotected sex that day. And you

said nothing since. And when you told Felipe that you were having a baby, I thought…I thought.'

'I'm sorry. My period came last week. I didn't tell you. We were barely talking and I didn't think you cared.'

No baby.

He strode aimlessly to the windows and stared blankly out of them.

She'd got her period.

She wasn't pregnant.

She'd thought he didn't care.

Why did he?

He'd tried not to. For the best part of a month he'd pretended he didn't care, but when he'd heard her tell Felipe that she was pregnant and realised that meant she would have to stay, he'd learned that he did care, more than he'd thought possible.

But no baby.

No child.

No son.

And that last grated more than the rest. He spun around. 'Do you ever tell the truth?'

'Alesander,' she appealed, 'please—'

'You've been spinning lies from the moment you arrived.'

'Yes, I've lied! All the time I've been here, I've been lying to Felipe and I hated myself for it, but there was a reason why I lied—good reason. Felipe was able to die happy because of those lies.'

'You probably don't even know how to tell the truth.'

'I told you the truth.'

'I don't think you're capable of it.'

'Alesander,' she said more firmly. 'I told you the truth.'

'But you said—'

'I said I love you.'

His eyes shuttered closed, his mind reeling back through their conversation. And she had said that, but he'd been blindsided by the words she hadn't said, by the words he'd been expecting, the words he'd grown used to since he'd first heard her utter them.

He hadn't had time to process these new ones.

'It was the truth. It is the truth. I'm only sorry it wasn't the truth you were wanting to hear.'

And they weren't the words he'd been expecting to hear, true.

But there was something in them, something that didn't bother him as much as he might have thought.

Something that resonated with him.

He didn't want her to go. He'd thought a baby would keep her here. He'd been devastated to know she wasn't pregnant, that she'd lied for Felipe when he'd wanted her words to be true.

There was no baby, but if she loved him, maybe there was a chance she still might stay.

'Do you have to go home to Australia?'

'What?'

'I know you have your studies to return to, but do you have to go? We have universities in Spain, after all. You could study here, finish your studies, improve your Spanish at the same time.'

Her heart leapt. What was he saying? She bit her lip, trying desperately not to read too much into his questions. There had been too many misunderstandings between them, too many times they had misunderstood each other and let each other down. 'Alesander?'

'Because if you do not need to leave, perhaps you could stay here, with me.'

'Even though I'm not pregnant?'

'Who says you're not? We had unprotected sex last night. I didn't think I needed to bother with a condom, under the circumstances. Only now I find the circumstances have changed and that perhaps you might be pregnant after all.'

'Oh.' Her heart sank. She'd been right not to get too excited. 'Oh, and you want me to wait. In case this time there's a baby.'

'Yes, of course I want any child of mine. But I want you too. I did not know that at first. I was determined to keep you here and when I heard that you were pregnant, it gave me a reason to make you stay. Because I want you here with me. Because I love you, Simone…'

She blinked.

'What did you say?'

'I said I love you. And I want you to stay. And we'll have unprotected sex as many times as it takes if it means you will.'

'Alesander…'

'I know I have not been easy to live with. I know I have treated you badly and that I have no right to ask for your love.'

Her heart was beating so fast it was all but tripping over itself, her smile was so wide it hurt and still she couldn't stop. 'You always told me not to make the mistake of thinking you were nice.'

'I am not nice. I am the first to admit it. But I will also admit that I am in love with you. Will you stay here in Spain with me, Simone? Will you stay and be my real wife and be the mother of my children? Will you stay and bear a son named Felipe and honour the memory of your grandfather? What do you say?'

'Oh yes,' she cried, her heart bursting with happiness. 'I say yes. I love you, Alesander, I love you so very much.'

And he smiled and took her into his arms and kissed her until she was giddy with joy.

'I love you too. I will always love you.'

EPILOGUE

Simone Esquivel went into labour nine months later, on a warm autumn night where the vine leaves rustled on the breeze up the trellised slopes and where the wine grapes grew fat on the view over the spectacular coastline.

It was exactly one year since the day she'd arrived on Alesander's doorstep and delivered her crazy proposal, a year that had changed like the seasons, and been filled with despair and loss, and hope and renewal.

And like the vines themselves, ancient and strong and with roots eighty feet deep, love had featured through it all.

Alesander was more nervous than Simone, fussing and fretting as he tried to manoeuvre her into first the car, and then into the hospital, as if he were trying to herd the sheep that grazed between the vines.

And when Simone refused to be herded and told him to calm down, he tried to herd the staff instead, barking out orders and demands so that nobody was in any doubt that the Esquivel baby was arriving tonight.

He held her hand while she laboured and fretted, and barked orders some more. He sponged her brow and moistened her lips and rubbed her back when she needed him to. And when their baby was born he watched in wonder and awe at this strong woman who he loved deliver him a son.

'You didn't lie to him,' he said later, as he sat by her side, his finger given over to the clutches of their tiny child, clearly besotted by their new son.

She must have looked as if she didn't understand.

'To Felipe. That last time you spoke to him before he died. You told him the truth. You told him you were having a baby and that you would have a son and we would name him Felipe.

'Don't you see,' he said, 'our baby was conceived that night. You spoke the truth.'

She smiled at him, this man who was her husband, who she had married to make an old man happy but who had given her his heart and this child and who now was giving her yet another precious gift.

'Thank you,' she said. 'Did I ever tell you I loved you, Alesander Esquivel?'

'You did,' he told her, 'but I didn't believe you then.' He leaned over the child they had made and kissed her ever so preciously on the lips.

'But I'll never doubt you again.'

* * * * *